ALLIANCE

Metamorphosis

A Novel of the Indigenous Americas

David Oliver ~ Godric

Alliance

METAMORPHOSIS

David Oliver-Godric

Alliance—Metamorphosis

This is a work of fiction. All the characters and events portrayed in this book are fictional, and any resemblance to real people or incidents is purely coincidental.

TABLE OF CONTENTS

Acknowledgements and Appreciation

Nanc Rick, my beloved and long-suffering wife: For putting up with me lost in the story for years, making me eat, sleep, etc., and being my first beta reader as the pages appeared on the screen.

Susan Uttendorfsky: For editing that saved this story when I got stuck—*really stuck*!

George Lepine, Okichitaw Combat Arts: For brilliant advice on aboriginal weapons and tactics.

Jane Freidman: For words of wisdom from an industry POV.

Pam Pederson: For first editing, encouragement, and cheerleading.

All the folks at Fiction Writers and Editors on Facebook: For always being happy to provide feedback.

Gina Peters: For moral support, encouraging the consumption of Butter Chicken, and help with the cover design.

Chief Clem Seymour, Seabird Band: For giving me a thumbs-up early on.

Andrea Toth: For early reading and encouragement.

Sandi Goodrich: For being a wise and early supporter and cheerleader.

All of my readers, Facebook, LinkedIn, and Blogger friends: Thank you!

Seabird Island Band: For giving me the opportunity to work with the amazing people who inspired this story.

Prologue

An Elder, Keeper of Stories, sits in a circle of young people. In an arc around her, children and youths, some of different appearance from the Keeper, watch her every gesture. Her skin has an earthy reddish hue. Among the young are some with skin like the color of bone and rounder, flatter faces. A few are a darker brown with narrow faces who sit next to taller youths whose long yellow hair rises above the rest. A fire crackles and pops in the center of the lodge, casting shadows that seem to be alive themselves. She speaks quietly, her voice powerful and gentle at the same time, and the listeners lean in to catch every word and gesture as her hands help weave the story:

"This tale is told in whispers among the Grassland People, when it is told at all. The River People tell it out loud and with a dignified touch of pride. Perhaps more than a touch. Many songs now sung in the lodges come from this time, so that we do not forget…

"Both communities contributed to the great deeds that were done, both contributed a key player to the events. The secret lies in the honor, and lack of it, that certain persons brought to the front when evil walked up on them. A man, or woman, is remembered for their doing. Those who do nothing are best forgotten, as that is what they have earned.

"A tall man, who is remembered, sets out from one end of a trail. A tall woman, nearly as tall as the man, who is also remembered, starts out at a far place on the same trail. This story happened between, and at both ends, and so it begins…"

Chapter 1: Hawk Blazes

Late Spring on a mountainside of the northwest coast of a previously undiscovered continent to the east of Song China, 1031 CE.

I see the flicker of an ear. The young buck blends perfectly with the hillside as he nibbles a berry bush below us on the hillside and I freeze. Carefully, slowly, I raise one finger wetted to the knuckle and feel a slight chill on the right side. It's only a soft breeze twisting as it rises up the hillside, carrying the earthy smell of the high mountains above us, but even that will push an arrow in flight. Sun-warmed hillsides are notorious for vagrant swirls and rushes as the air flows through hollow nooks and protruding crags. Lining up the shot, I hold my breath, then hear the faint *thud* of the bowstring, lost as soon as the arrow leaves the bow. The buck drops, snagging on the bush he nibbled on. Two figures move as quickly as they dare down the slope to secure it.

Seabird grasps one of the deer's hind legs and Boomer grabs the other. Together they drag the carcass up to a flat hollow where we camped. The slope below is jagged stone sentinels surrounded by steep loose scree with scattered shrubs. The odd scrub cedar clings tenaciously to old ice cracks in the still-solid rock.

We skin and gut the carcass, empty the organ cavity, and pack it with salt. I strip the intestines of their contents and pack the tubes with the organs into the cavity, leaving aside the liver and heart as our hunters' portion. Boomer cuts the legs off of the torso and wraps the whole carcass inside the hide, securing the bundle with supple buckskin straps.

Boomer builds a small fire to roast the heart and liver on green branches, a good sear, and shares out the chunks as they cook. After our meal, Seabird buries the fire and covers the spot with dirt and detritus. We maintain a strict silence with fresh meat in the camp. Too many hunters tell stories of a cougar, lynx, or bear walking in on a fresh kill. Done with our meal, we sweep the site with dead branches, scatter leaves and twigs over the area. Predators will smell the blood, but we'll be long gone.

Before we leave, I survey the valley below. Branches sway in the breeze rising up the sun-warmed stone face. A flash seizes my attention—white inner bark glows on a dark hemlock where someone has marked the spot. We mark useful trails with blazes by cutting out a strip of dark outer bark, which exposes the young white inner bark. With a hatchet, you create a blaze quickly: two strikes, top and bottom, then two on the sides and strip the outer bark away. Sometimes rows of angle cuts add information, such as destination or purpose. In dappled flickers of sunlight, blazes shine like the moon on a dark night.

This might only be wind damage, or a rockfall skinned it, so I look the other way. An identical flash of inner bark glows here too—another beacon against the darker forest. Nothing moves at the moment, so my neck relaxes a bit and I stretch it out, side to side, before speaking.

"Fresh trail blazes—not ours. These are wide, like they don't care about the tree. Bugs will be in the bark come Spring."

Boomer rumbles a soft growl as only he can produce with his massive chest.

"Intrusion? We've suffered no drought. Food shortages might drive intrusion, but food abounds." His face hardens, grim like a spirit mask and as hard as the stones we stand on.

Normally carefree Seabird scowls. "No raids have struck for many lifetimes. Rain is plentiful for our neighbors, the salmon thick enough in the creek and River runs that a hunter can walk across their backs to cross."

I shrug, having no answers. I hate that.

Caution foremost in our minds, we slip back from the ledge and take cover behind a clump of young hemlock trees, out of sight from all directions, our speech muffled.

Boomer notes, "That's a wide trail, as if for many warriors."

Both of us sign AGREE.

Seabird leans forward. "I'll build a sledge and take the meat back to the village. Boomer will watch your back better than me."

Boomer nudges my arm and smirks. Seabird's curled lip betrays him, and I can't resist raising an eyebrow as I cock my head toward Boomer. "Yes, he wants to be the hero with supper. Maybe for that Willow girl?"

Seabird straightens, adopts a stern frown, and rolls his eyes. "Keep up—it's Woodfern this week. Willow likes to sit around the house all the time. I can do that for a little while, but all day, every day?" He shrugs and droops sadly. Boomer and I shake our heads and smile.

We build the sledge together: two poles tied together in an apex, a spreader pole holding the base wide apart, cross-laced with more straps to support the load. Then we strap on the hide bundle for the trip.

Seabird sets off west on our trail back to Fishcamp. Boomer and I watch him disappear out of sight, then start down into the densely forested valley. Flakes of heavy scree slide under unwary feet, so we pick our way carefully through the skirt of treacherous loose stone, peeled from the higher peaks. Rain and snowmelt expands in cracks during Winters, splitting the flakes away from the Mother stone.

It takes some time to reach the first blaze. The bottomland, nourished by minerals from decomposing stone and many streams, grows thick with willow, dogwood, varied ferns, and berry bushes. Walking around to the other side of the tree, I find the expected second blaze, about as high as an average person easily reaches with a hatchet. It too shines bright and fresh.

"Yes, they marked both sides. Given the size of the area cleared for the trail, they expect many people will travel this frequently."

Boomer's fists clench, his face reddens. I agree with his feelings. He peers west, toward home. "I see one, two... Then it turns."

I sigh. "You follow those back west to Fishcamp or Highwater. Tell Chief Fisheagle what we've found. This trail must lead somewhere, so I'll run the trail east for one day, then wait for you for three days. Look for three stones on the north side of the trail. If you don't come, I'll come looking for you, with help."

Boomer's jaw muscles bulge and fade like a pulse. "Yes."

He vanishes around a bend. Fast but silent as can be, I ghost beneath the trees, alert for any unusual sight or sound. I stop for water three times. Crouched in a squat with my head up, I bring the water to my mouth so I won't miss any movement. In the valley bottom, the brush thickens, but clearly visible signs suggest a party of at least twenty. I search for each next blaze and take note of signs on the trail.

Surprisingly, I spot a bit of leather, moccasin scuffs, scars where someone has kicked stones. The brush cuts are as fresh as the blazes. Running trail freely, I cover much more ground in less time than if I were bushwhacking, and a lot of forest passes behind me by sundown.

As the light fades into dusk, I turn off the trail and make a simple camp in a cozy meadow screened from the trail by a long thicket of willows. A gravel-bottomed stream supplies clean water and I carry a bag of dried meat and fruit, but I don't want to dip into it yet, so I forage while waiting. Exploring the meadow, I harvest some herbs and mushrooms and shoot a squirrel out of a cottonwood tree. This will tide me over until I hunt tomorrow.

The night is uneventful. Waking early, I hide all traces of my camp before caching my supplies high in the branches of a cedar tree. My scent will scare off most scavengers. A raccoon could find it. Maybe a crow or raven, but it is the best choice for now. I explore the open meadow in hopes of finding greens and roots. I eat my fill of fresh greens and still have a bag full of various starchy roots for the next run. I consider hunting or fishing but decide we have enough for the two of us to carry if we need to move fast and quiet. We will find more meadows.

The next day dawns clear and warm, though high wispy clouds suggest it won't last, particularly as it blows moisture inland from the coast. A piece of venison jerky soothes my hunger as I indulge in some reflection: I don't like to wait—I think too much and worry. All the local communities are friends and we trade with many others from much farther away, but mostly west and south across the River. The trade is profitable for both parties, and I cannot imagine any of them trying to move into River People territory. We potlatch together and many send courting parties. We have received the same, so it makes no sense.

Reliable Boomer will return as soon as he can, so to keep busy, I make a small rain shelter at the edge of the meadow. A big fir tree has blown down—ripped its roots out of the earth, leaving a cozy hollow behind. I cut and strip willow stems to weave a frame over the pit, then cover that with fern fronds, followed by bigleaf maple leaves to shed rainwater. Finally, I cover the whole thing with mulch and dirt from the forest floor.

I also gather bundles of long grass and more ferns from the far side of the meadow. These I place inside the pit to soften the stones in the bottom. The forest looks untouched. Satisfied, I scout the back trail a short way, thinking Boomer is about due. I catch a faint sound and slide behind a nearby tree. I peek around the other side, low to the ground.

"Hah!" Seabird pops out of a nearby thicket. "You used to be good at hide-and-seek. What happened?"

"Humph. I heard you a long way back."

"No, you didn't."

Grinning and glad to see him, I grab his arm in greeting.

He cocks his head with pride. "You've got to admit the sneak into that bush was good."

I flash an enigmatic smile. "Did you cross trails with Boomer?"

"He was at Fishcamp, on his way to Highwater. He should be here soon."

"Good! I've had enough of waiting. I made a hide, and I've gathered some traveling food. I thought you were going to stay and look after Woodfern. Did she figure out you were only after a little fun?" I throw in a questioning eyebrow lift.

"Woodfern? It's Copperflower this week."

"It's only been two days since it was Woodfern, most of which you were traveling."

"She's a smart one, always coming up with projects and errands for me. Copperflower is much more relaxed about stuff like that… It worries me sometimes. Have you seen anything?"

"All quiet. If three of us are traveling, we should look for some more food."

"Copperflower sent along some bannock and berries and we can travel quite a way on that." He pats the bulging bag slung over his shoulder.

"I know she makes the best bannock. You're not the only wolf on the prowl."

Seabird's right eyebrow arcs up, too far to be serious. "Do we fight after we save the People and stop whatever this bunch is up to?"

"No. I'll wait a week and move in!"

"Yeah, that'd probably work." He chuckles, then heaves a resigned sigh. "Show me your cache and I'll put the food in it."

***

Boomer arrives as the sun starts its slide into evening and delivers his news. "The blazes turn north to the east of Highwater, hugging the base of the valley wall. They're keeping clear of settlements, so I think they're scouting and setting up for raids. I don't like that at all."

I shake my head. "Traders don't avoid settlements." I beckon them to follow me to the cache, where we divide up supplies, then sweep the area with branches and toss them on the hide. A careful search might turn up signs of our occupancy, but from the trail, everything looks natural. It's time to seek answers to our questions, so we set out to follow the blazes to whatever is at the other end.

We note scuffs and disturbed stones as we run. Also, bits of food dropped and now covered with ants, chewed sticks discarded when they lost their flavor, even a scrap of leather thong—all signs of a large party passing. Whoever it is, they're not being very careful. We agree they appear to be at least twenty, moving fast.

The trail leads us on, day after day, and the signs slowly grow fresher. The weather holds, makes tracking easy, even without the blazes along the route. The sun rises, miles pass. The sun sets, and still we press on each day until dark. We hunt and forage as we need.

***

A week passes, then two. Well out of our home territory, the trail turns north, following the River. We swim across to the east side as it turns north and exits a steep narrow canyon. To the west, a sheer wall of stone rises high above us. The east side is a mix of stone and cut bank, much closer to the water. Any earlier in the season and we would have had to backtrack for days to a place we could build a canoe.

We discover a lone canoe hidden where the intruders likely crossed. Confirming our suspicions, we land in a quiet cove where a trail leads up the stony bank. Several canoes lay bottom up on trestles at the top of the bench above the flood cut. Large coils of rope clearly show how they are raised and lowered to cross the River. I draw some comfort that all but one of the canoes are on the northbound trail side.

The trail continues to climb for a day, but once past the narrow canyon, with its raging rapids, the River widens—now placid in comparison—and the land turns to dry rounded grassy hills dotted with gray tufty plants and very dry grasses. Crushing a tough, narrow leaf of a tufty plant, we recognize the pungent smell that confirms it is a kind of sage we take in trade to burn in ceremonies.

We all begin to wonder if the trail will ever end. One critical question plagues us: Why have these strangers come so far? What can be worth this kind of time and effort? Traders tend to be solitary, or teams of two or three at most, and they know and follow the existing trails. It's the recurring topic of conversation every night as we sit around the fire. It doesn't make sense, unless it is all preparation for an invasion.

Chapter 2: Midnight Awakening

I stand out from most of the girls and women in my village. Taller than most men, slender, my hair worn in long black braids decorated with strings of colored beads and bits of hammered copper woven in on thin sinew strings, I wear the tanned buckskin vest and half pants I prefer in Summer. I've seen fourteen summers and sinewy muscles ripple along my reddish-brown arms and legs as I move and bring to life my tattoos: the traditional salmon, a soaring hawk, and my favorite—a fat raccoon. My breasts are smaller than most of the girls', but I understand that will change when I have children.

Our village is one of many on the Syilx Plateau. My father came from the vast plains across the Great Mountains when he was about my age. It is how the chiefs keep our communities from growing too large for the amount of food the land can give us. It also brings new blood to our villages. Usually the young men go to other communities because girls sometimes die in childbirth, so young men are traditionally in surplus.

I yearn for something. I love my family, the Chief, and most of the people in our village, but our Shaman scares me. He goes on about how we must do better and claims that the spirits are unhappy with us. He criticizes everything; no peace exists in the man. I think he has some bad spirit living in him who eats all his happiness and grinds at his heart, if he has one, but I see no sign of that.

Oftentimes I wish I could travel to other places, like the traders do, because they must see all sorts of exciting things. Perhaps that will be my vocation. The

Elders say that many spirits live in sacred places throughout the land. I have not seen any spirits, but I believe the Elders—they exist.

Nosey is heavy, but my shoulder is used to the raccoon's weight for short distances. I found him staggering along two years ago, torn and bloody from a desperate fight with something, and nursed him back to his present pudgy health. He has been my constant companion since, mostly to my delight. To balance my occasional annoyance, he backed off a starved coyote last Winter who saw a meal in me. He ran up an overhanging tree as I held the gaunt animal back with my staff. Nosey scrambled out on a limb and dropped onto the coyote's back, all claws and teeth! The coyote didn't survive the two of us, but he did make a nice pelt that Nosey claimed as his nest after it was cleaned and softened.

We come to my family's house and I scramble up the side of the dried mud dome to the smokehole and the slanted, notched pole that sticks up out of it. I hold my breath as I climb down and pass through the smoke. The pole is high enough that it doesn't burn; it hardens over time. When we reach the floor, dug out to about my height from ground level, Nosey jumps down and waddles to his coyote pelt for a nap.

***

A while later, I hear shouting outside and scurry up the pole to investigate. *The scouts are back*! A group of hunters left almost two moons ago and no one seems to know why, except the Chief—or the Elders who sent them—and they aren't telling. Everyone I've spoken to assumes that they scout new hunting grounds, but they carry nothing except their weapons and grub bags. I expect them to report to the Chief's house, but they head straight to the Shaman's house. My curiosity runs wild.

I rise the rest of the way out of my house, slide down, and wander innocently over to the Shaman's pit house. All I hear is unintelligible murmuring through the thick wattle and mud, so I move around to the treed side and cautiously creep up to the smokehole. The voices rise clearly now—one of the hunters describes a village. I don't recognize it as any of the villages I know. It must be far away, which makes sense given how long the hunters have been gone.

The Shaman asks questions in his raspy, crackling voice. "What's the hunting like?"

Hardspear answers. "The land flourishes, lush and green. Game animals swarm in the woodlands. The streams are alive with food fish! Deer, bear, moose, all are fat and common. Salmon and trout teem in a multitude of rivers, streams, and lakes. Plump marmots and many other animals and birds throng on land and in water. We followed the River to the coast, avoided contact with the locals as you instructed. If we are successful, we will always have food."

Shaman giggles—hisses, "Yesss!"

It sounds like a land I would dream of in the long, hot dry of a Syilx Summer.

Shaman continues. "What about people? Are they many?"

Hardspear sniggers. "Many small villages, some widely separated. We suggest several could be taken at the same time, if we can gather enough hunters."

My eyes flare wide; my hand flies to my mouth to seal it. *They speak of war*! War between the peoples in our lands has not occurred for lifetimes. Old stories tell about raids for slaves, but that has mostly died out. Sometimes we raid for animals or food when times are hard, but this is something new—raiding for territory when we have full storerooms. This has been a good year, so far. Our People live where they always have. They live and die in balance, mostly; if food is scarce, or too many babies come for our land to provide for, then some youngsters are sent to villages that need people. Others go off exploring and find new homes, or they are eaten by a bear or something.

Shaman has always been strange. They say that he came to us alone from the high mountains in his sixteenth year. Our old Shaman died when a cloudburst suddenly swelled a stream he was standing in atop a high cliff. The young visitor said the spirits took him as a sign that we needed new guidance. He proclaimed himself Shaman, having supposedly communed with the ancestors and the great spirits of the land. We accepted that, having no reason not to. In the five years since, he has become a strong voice in the community and influences many decisions of the Chief and council.

Anger rises in my heart. The stories of the old wars are very clear about what "war" means. People die on both sides. Men, women, children; old and young. Both sides take slaves. Villages burn. The memories of the People die forever along with the Elders. The land itself, our Mother, will be burned and scarred. My mind whirls. Thoughts come to me and I dismiss them. Some hold possibilities, and I keep those aside. Slowly, a plan of action begins to form.

I have always walked my own paths. I know I am unusual among the People, who keep busy with family and friends. I contribute, but spend much of my time on the land, happy with Nosey and the wild animals for company. Some of the hunters have tried to be overly friendly to me, but I have never felt more than a spark with any of them, and some bear scars from being demanding. I love my family and the Grassland People, but always feel most comfortable by myself. Now I need advice—and some wisdom—before I act.

The obvious choice is my mother first. It feels safest, and my mother is wise in her years. My father is working. I glance around, but no one takes any interest, so I slide down Shaman's house as quietly as I can and stride quickly, purposefully to my family's home. My luck is good—she sings her berry song as she cleans and prepares them for drying and storage.

Fall nears, and storing food is the priority for most of the village. I wonder for a moment how much smoked meat is in the community larder, with so many hunters gone scouting for so long. Each family keeps a stock from what they harvest, but part normally goes to our village stores.

Running to her, I burst into tears, wrap my arms around her, and surrender to my emotions for a moment. Then I pull away and look directly into my mother's eyes.

"The Shaman readies us for war."

Mama Coolwater's eyebrows shoot halfway to her hairline, her eyes growing big and round. Now I know she was unaware of the Shaman's plans. I wonder how many others haven't been told.

"I heard him talking to the hunters who got back a short time ago—with no meat. They have been scouting for all this time, somewhere to the west. They found villages of people in a rich land where the sage and prickly plants don't grow and rain comes often, sometimes even in Summer. Shaman wants us to take their villages, food, and people for our own. The people who live on those lands will be slaves. I heard it!"

We stand still, facing each other for a few minutes while she thinks. Her eyes scrunch as they always do when she really puzzles at something serious.

"Sit," she says, pushing a bowl of berries at me. I obey and absently take a few and begin chomping on them. Nosey awakened from his nap when I came back into the house. He senses my distress, watching me closely, then stretches and ambles over to sit at my feet, his alert eyes scanning all around.

Time passes and Mama Coolwater says nothing. I begin to shift impatiently. Still she stares at the walls, silent.

Abruptly, she thumps her hands flat on the table and fixes her eyes on mine. "You would do something about this?"

"Yes, I must. The deaths, the suffering… Why do we need more land? Why can we not trade with them for things we want? The days of warriors, instead of hunters, are long in the past. We know this land, and its spirits care for us. We do not know the spirits of their lands. It's an evil plan that our People will pay a price for. Our spirits, even our ancestors, may turn against us if we do this. It is wrong! I know this with my whole body and mind."

"Hush, daughter, I hear you. Listen for a moment."

I nod, reaching down to stroke Nosey, who nuzzles my leg softly.

"I will go to the Chief. I will ask if he knows about this plan and if he approves of it." She smiles reassuringly, but I sense that she is not looking forward to challenging the Chief, who we assume has approved this war. I grab her hand with both of my own, my thankfulness reflecting in her eyes.

A scream erupts outside, then shouting and wails. Both of us spring to our feet, turn to the step pole, and I scramble up with Mama right on my heels. As my head clears the smokehole, everyone is running toward the Chief's house and a growing column of smoke.

Chapter 3: Hawk Murder

The trail ends. Not the trail itself, which has become more and more obvious and travel-worn, but we pass the last blazed tree. No more are seen in any direction.

I glance at Boomer and Seabird. "We're close."

They both raise a hand to show they hear, still scanning the bush around them. The vegetation here is not at all what we are used to. Coastal rainforest has given way to dry inland desert, the trees from cedar, hemlock, and maples to pine, with tufts of dryland sage. We have traveled over mountain ranges, through long valleys, and have crossed many streams and a couple of small rivers where the water shallowed out over gravel bars. We are lucky it is late in the Summer and water levels are low. In Spring, those bodies of water will be impassable, judging by the erosion and the rocks scoured of any moss or other vegetation.

We have a short time to reconnoiter the area before heading back home or we'll be stuck here in a strange, and probably dangerous, territory as Fall sets in and the snows come. The need to discover what's going on and report back quickly drives us on. It could still be that this trip is for nothing, that no threat exists.

Boomer smells it first. "Smoke!"

"Which way?"

We scan the sky. I taste the acrid scent now.

"That way." Seabird points to a wisp in the sky to the northeast. We've been heading more or less north for about a half a moon, two seven-days, working our way up a deep River valley that widened into long narrow lakes in places. The land has forced some untimely detours, but we've mostly been able to move fast and far.

In a ground-eating long stride we run toward the smoke and it grows thicker and darker. We begin to hear shouts, and flames glow in the haze. Our cover thins as we approach what is clearly a large village. We move from bush to boulder, dropping into hollows, carefully working our way closer.

As the brush thins further, near the odd-shaped houses, we spread apart, each making our own way. I spot a clump of thick willows that I think will give me cover and a clear sightline toward the source of the fire. After working my way into the middle of it, I see people running to and from the fire, likely with bags of water. It involves one structure—a larger version of the smaller houses around it. Almost everyone is trying to put the fire out with water and dirt.

A lone body lies stretched on the ground a short way from the burning house, and two women bend over it. A scrawny man approaches the body on the ground and the two women. He's completely covered in tattoos and wears looped strings of stone and bone. A headband supports strings of crow feathers, and a stained loincloth wraps around his waist.

"Shaman!" I whisper, shocked when one of the women, the younger one, rises and screams at the Shaman, throwing dirt and stones at him.

Smoke swirls. It hides, then reveals. The spirit-walker turns and runs to a rickety shed. The two women near the body now hold each other while the young one sobs. They move off together and disappear down the notched log of another one of the pit houses.

I slowly shake my head, wondering. *Clearly, something important is happening besides the fire. No one yells at a Shaman, let alone pelts one with dirt and stones.* He, or she, is the spiritual heart of a community, and usually the healer for sicknesses of body, mind, and spirit.

I watch people battle the fire for a short time more, and then slither out of the willow thicket, scurrying in a spider run, bent over on all fours, away from the village. I move straight toward the riverbank, trusting Seabird and Boomer to follow. I desperately want to find out what they make of this. I slide down a cut bank marking high water and wait.

My mind goes over and over what I saw. All I have is questions, no answers.

I risk a peek over the bank and catch a flash of movement upstream. A moment later, Boomer comes around the bend and sinks into a squat next to me, his eyes wide and his mouth a grim straight line, tense at the corners. Seabird appears from downstream and settles next to us.

Boomer is the first to speak. "Murder."

Seabird agrees. "That's what it looks like, and I think the Shaman is the main suspect...to the girl, anyway."

I nod. "My read as well. Then someone torched the house to hide it. I'd bet the women pulled him out." The others nod. "We'll watch for a while. Maybe we'll find an opportunity to grab a wanderer and gain some information on what's going on here." Boomer and Seabird agree.

Alliance—Metamorphosis

Chapter 4: Midnight Flight

Back in our house, Mother and I hug each other tightly. Then she pushes me back, gripping my arms.

"Shaman won't hide for long. He must take control of this situation to establish himself as Chief. You hurt his pride and challenged him in his moment of triumph—unforgivable actions. What will you do?"

I consider, but my mind isn't focused. It spins like a dust demon and I take a deep breath, trying to settle myself. "I cannot challenge him with the hunters supporting him."

Mama Coolwater nods and smiles encouragingly, clearly waiting for more.

"I was the one who threw dirt and stones at him. He should have no reason to harm you, or Father. You can spread the truth quietly here. I must leave, or I'll have some 'accident' that might hurt you both." I draw a deep breath. "I will warn the villages that Shaman wants to take over."

A pang of fear strikes: of the journey, of being alone, of meeting strangers who will have every reason to think me insane for the tale I bring. I have never been far from home, but…

"I must do this. Others deserve a warning."

"That's my daughter! I know how to pack for you. Bring warm clothes fit for Winter because you'll be outside when the cold comes. Then have a cuddle with Nosey. He's upset because you are, and he doesn't know why, or what's coming. You can slip out to the River, wait for dark, then head south and toward the setting sun as you can. Look for trail blazes—the hunters will have marked the way."

I look down at my moccasins. "Thank you, Mother. I fear leaving the other good people here. I don't believe everyone approves of the war. If I can, I will come back for you if I find a safe place for us." My jaw muscles bulge and release. "I will not fail."

Turning away, I begin pulling my winter gear out of its storage space, then stop to give Nosey a reassuring scratch on my way to change and grab what I want to take.

By the time I return, Mama has brought out a packboard my father uses for carrying game. She has attached bags of food for the journey and more little bags of things that she knows I will need, then wraps a blanket around the whole thing. It has taken the hunters over two moons to make the trip, with extra time to scout their prey. It will be a long time before I can possibly return. Knowing that I will be on the trail for at least a moon, I grab my stack of moon-time cloths and add a few personal items to remind me of home.

We finish lashing everything tight. Dressed in supple brown buckskin—a sleeved shirt and pants—I should be warm and protected from branches and brambles.

"Keep houses between you and the Shaman's house. Move fast to the River, then go downstream a bit until you can't hear or see the village and wait for dusk. Then head downriver until you find the hunters' trail. You know the marks to look for."

We hug, then she helps me hoist the pack on and settle it. I touch her face and climb the pole out of my home, Nosey following close behind. I scan for anyone watching. No one looks my way, so I ease down the side away from Shaman's house, bend over, and waddle low like the ducks do to the River. I slide over the bank…

…right into the arms of three strange men. I try to stop—to shove myself back up the bank. They are stronger and drag me back.

I struggle hard against three of them. One of the strangers has a hand over my mouth, as if I would call anyone here to help. Another holds me in place by the shoulders while Nosey gnaws on his ankle. The third squats, ready for me to make a break in any direction.

I realize that Nosey could be hurt or killed if I keep struggling, so I stop still and raise my arms, palms up, to show they are empty. The man covering my mouth slowly takes his hand away. The one holding my shoulders lets go and removes Nosey from his now-bloody ankle. He tosses him toward me and I reach out for Nosey. He runs up my back to a shoulder, still baring his red dripping fangs at the strangers. He shakes his head vigorously, which throws a spray of crimson drops in all directions.

"Can you understand me?" one asks.

"Yes. You sound strange, but your speech is like our trade tongue."

"Good! Why are you packed for a long journey?"

I look at him and questions writhe in my mind: *Who are they? Why did they hide so close to the village? Very well...*

"Quickly, tell me who you are."

"Hawk," the tall one says as he points to himself. "Boomer, and Seabird." He nods toward each of the others. "We are River People. Our lands and villages begin a moon's run south and west of here and we followed a wide, new trail that led us here. We need to know why your people scout our territory."

Hawk stops speaking and a rush of evening wind begins to stir the dry grasses of Summer's end. It's a soft welcoming to the close of a harsh day as the sun touches the western mountains and begins his slow slide to his resting place to wait for morning in the east. In that light, I search the faces of the strong young hunters and their eyes look straight into mine. They have restrained, but not threatened me, and now freedom lies in my hands.

"I have a story you must hear, but we are not at a safe place to tell it."

The big one called Boomer smiles. "I think we've found what we need."

Hawk looks back to the south. "We must be far from here before we camp. I do not want to be surprised if they come looking for the woman."

"My name is Midnight."

"Midnight." Hawk nods to me, and so do the others. I return their acknowledgement of me as a person.

"Seabird, wrap your ankle—we don't want a blood trail. Boomer, would you take her pack?"

"I can carry it!"

"I know you can," Hawk says, "but you have to deal with that furry ball of teeth. Boomer will move quickly with the pack. We have a long run ahead."

"All right, for now." I slide from the straps and hand the pack to the big one, Boomer. He tries it on, then shrugs it off and adjusts the straps as Seabird finishes tying a strip of cloth tightly over a pad of moss from the riverbank to stop any infection on his ankle. Hawk finds a wind-broken branch to wipe out all signs of our passing.

Boomer heads off, setting the pace, followed by Seabird and myself. We aim for the treeline and Hawk catches up as we reach it and motions me over to him.

"You know this area. The trail we followed ends over here." He points to the edge of the trees. "It goes south about three days' travel, then angles west at a tall craggy mountain. Can we take another way to reach that area?"

"Not here. The valley is long and narrow. We have to cross the River at the gravel bar, a day south, if you want to go west."

He nods. "That's where we crossed. Will they search for you?"

I think for a few moments. "I shamed the Shaman, so yes, sooner or later."

The River men grin. Seabird says, "We saw."

"He is angry, but he had the Chief killed, or did it himself!"

The men's eyes narrow, glance at each other, then focus again on me and I continue. "He will first make sure of his power over the village. I know good people here who will have nothing to do with war. We should have a few days before they realize I follow the trail. I have family to the north and east, farther up the plateau, so he would expect me to go to them, I think… Oh, I hope they don't hurt my parents." The last is a fervent whisper.

Hawk flicks his head up, then downstream. "We will talk more tonight. For now, let's go." He takes off, quickly settling into a ground-eating stride. I follow last, after I settle Nosey on my shoulder. He can move fast for short distances, but he is no long-distance runner.

After a while, my shoulder starts to cramp from Nosey's weight on the one side and I call a halt. "Bring my pack."

Boomer comes over, shrugs off the pack, and sets it next to me. I untie the top and dig around inside a bit. I find a strong buckskin bag and some leather straps. Working quickly, I attach the straps to the bag and the bag to the pack. Then I put Nosey inside and adjust the pack straps to fit my shoulders and shrug the whole thing onto my back. Nosey pokes his head out and chirps contentment. Boomer shrugs, nods, and we take off again.

The mountains here rise higher and steeper to the northwest than they have been: sheer faces of rock with ledges and crevasses that support islands of shrubs and fir trees between the barren cliffs. The bases of these stone walls are jumbles of scree: chunks of the massifs split from the faces by rainwater that seeps into any small crevice and expands as it freezes. In the Spring thaw, the falling flakes are a hazard. At this time of year, only a few rivulets track like trails of tears down the dry gray-brown crags.

We run through the evening and after, through the darkness. Hawk seems able to see the trail ahead, and we stay close to him. I sense him somehow, so we carry on.

Hawk finally stops. "We rest here. Eat, sleep, and leave at dawn. No fire tonight. I want to put some distance between us and that village. But we also need to talk."

I slide out of the pack, and Hawk smiles at my expression of relief. "I'll take the pack tomorrow." I don't argue.

We eat dried meat and I contribute berries. While we eat, we talk, and Hawk tells the story about finding the blazed trail, his suspicions, and then the long run up the trail to the village. Afterward, I tell my story: How the hunters returned empty-handed and went to the Shaman's house instead of the Chief's; how I crept up to the smokehole, and what I heard; and how I told my mother what I knew and what I planned.

Hawk seems impressed. "You have honor, and courage. So does your mother."

Embarrassed by his praise, I look away. "I simply thought it was the right thing to do."

Hawk smiles. "Enough for tonight. Seabird, first watch, then me, then Boomer."

I bristle, annoyed because they aren't treating me as part of the team. I want to put a stop to it as quickly as possible. "I can take a watch, too!"

Hawk glances at his friends, considering for a moment. "Very well. Short watches, then, with Midnight third. We leave at dawn."

***

I rise and stretch as the sky lightens to a bright, shiny new day, and take a few moments to look at the three men I have fallen in with. They're all young—about twenty winters, I guess—strongly muscled with a few small scars visible on arms and legs. Boomer has a healed notch in one earlobe.

Seabird shows four parallel ridges on one arm where something clawed him in the past. Cougar…or bobcat, perhaps. The scars are not large enough for bear. I've seen bear scars, and I run hard when I stumble onto one of the unpredictable giants. The men have light blankets they wear folded, slung across the top left shoulder down to the right waist—even Seabird, who I've noticed favors his left—tied with straps during the day. Now they are bare above the waist, even Boomer, who's sitting last watch.

I admire the magnificent tattoos on their chests and arms. Hawk has a stylized bird of prey—an osprey, perhaps, with outstretched wings across his back and shoulders. Three wide, angled black bars are spaced down the outside of both upper arms and legs. In a shadowy forest, that would help break up his silhouette.

The sky lightens to blue-gray and I smell pine in the fresh morning air. I reach over to Hawk and touch his arm. He wakes instantly, looks at me for a moment, and smiles. Then he rolls and touches Seabird, who also wakes clear-eyed. A nearby creek burbles cheerily as we take turns splashing our faces and arms to rinse off the trail dust while the others keep watch. Refreshed, I swing my packboard up on my back and settle it. Hawk smiles. *My pack, my choice.*

Nosey drinks from the creek, and then some dried meat from Seabird seals the peace between them. The pace we travel is too fast for his short legs for any distance, so it is ride or be carried. Seabird lifts Nosey up to the bag and slides his back end and bushy tail into the bag, confirming my thought that they have bonded since our meeting. *Mutual esteem, perhaps.* The three strangers consistently display genuine respect to me as well.

We follow the River valley south to cut across the blazed trail, and they say we can follow that back to their home. The hunters from my village made quite the trail—much more obvious than I would have.

Chapter 5: Midnight Challenge

Late on the second day, Boomer spots a blaze a short way in front of us and gestures at it. He freezes and spins to face us, making downward slashing motion with both arms. Then he turns and walks calmly toward the blazed tree as two hunters come out of the woods next to it, headed straight for him. Hawk slides his bow out of its bindings and checks his hatchet at his waist. Seabird has his knife out and they run to Boomer. I drop my pack and Nosey bails out of his bag as it falls. The hunters spot us…belatedly. The woman unslings her bow, nocks an arrow, and the man unhooks a warclub from his belt as they trot toward us.

I streak past the Rivermen, Nosey charging along behind. I hold a large hunting knife in my right hand and a flint hatchet in my left. Abruptly, I stop and wait for my new companions, a broad toothy grin on my face at the hunters' confusion. They know me.

Puzzlement makes them stop, and each glances at the other.

"Midnight! Who are these men?" shouts one.

"They are old friends from up north. They trade and need to find the trail east. What are you two so jumpy about? Strangers are always welcome here."

The hunters look even more confused and whisper back and forth. One peers at my big pack, turns to the other, and shrugs. They put away their weapons and hold their hands out, open and raised. We do the same and gather together to talk.

I speak to the warriors first. "Fishhawk, Willowspear, these are friends of mine from upcountry. They trade to the east and south. Meet Hawk, Boomer, and Snowbird."

I catch Seabird's little twitch in the corner of my eye. I understand and he's smart enough to let it go. "Seabird" would be a dead giveaway of where he is from. "We hurry to make the south ford by dark."

The hunters nod. Then I press them further. "Why do you challenge strangers here?"

The Grasslanders look awkward—embarrassed, even. Willowspear's eyes focus down, where she scuffs the soil with one foot. Fishhawk's jaw clenches and unclenches as he invents a response.

"The Chief worries about raiders," Fishhawk finally says. "It is the time of year when we have the most food and other supplies gathered for Winter."

"But we are friends and family with all the villages and bands around here. It wasn't a bad year, so why does he think that would change?"

Now both aspirant warriors look even more uncomfortable. Then Fishhawk finds an easy answer. "You'll have to ask him. We only follow orders and we have to go now." He nods to us. "Good trading."

The two hunters turn, heading north toward the village. When they are out of hearing, the Rivermen and I let go great sighs. Nosey sits, watching.

I walk to the pack where I dropped it and wrestle it to an upright position. Nosey scrambles into his bag. Hawk gives it a boost as I hoist it onto my back again saying, "We had best put more distance between us and the village. They have obviously been out here since before I caused all the excitement back at the village. They'll report, and more hunters will come looking for answers to questions, and for me." I shiver, stand tall, and we set out again.

Chapter 6: Shaman Beginnings

I have seen it, the future! It comes to me in the dark, in gravid dreams. Warriors capture village after village in a lush and fertile land, and all that was theirs is mine.

The People of the Grasslands honor me and other tribes fear me. I will live forever in their songs. No one defies me, and many women lie with me and bear my children. THIS is a dream worth pursuing.

I was not born here. My parents lived on the plains beyond the Great Mountains to the east. I grew up during a cycle of harsh weather. Summers burned the grasses with heat and cooked all the water from the soil. Locusts devoured what was left, then the Winters came and blew the snow in swirls and clouds until you could not find your own feet, nor trails to follow. Many died in those years and all suffered, especially scrawny children. I resolved not to be one of them.

I learned to eat anything that might sustain me, and I did survive. But one day I was seen eating forbidden flesh and they ran me off the food with spears and hatchets. When I tried to return home, my own father told me to leave and never return.

I began to hate people that day, and during the many long days that came after. I also discovered the lesson of survival.

I have found a way to make my dream real. The People here listen to me. A few were convinced to go forth and search, and they have found my perfect lands on the way downriver, all the way to the Great Water.

More of the People listen now when I speak of much food, slaves to do their work, and warmer Winters. The chill that lives in my bones and mind will finally thaw when I make my new home in those warm lands downriver.

Chapter 7: Hawk
The Run for Home

Time and the trail go by quickly, and no more hunters from the Grasslands bother us. Rains occur more frequently now, soaking all of us and our gear. Midnight has the worst of it with her big pack. Seabird fashioned a rain shield that covers Nosey's bag while we took one of our rests. Winter comes—we feel the change as an ache in our bones at night, but running the trail loosens our muscles after a while.

During these long runs, I think about what I've learned. I don't believe Midnight's Shaman will attack this close to snowfall. His people hadn't looked ready, and it will take too much time to prepare. They need to make arrows and other weapons over the Winter and trade for extra foodstuffs for the journey, even if they count on plunder at the end of the trail. In Spring, when the wild winds and rains slow down…then they will come.

If they were a raiding people, like those I have heard of from the big Grasslands far to the east and the south, I would worry that they follow right on our heels. But they are not—their "warriors" are hunters who have turned their arms to strange game. They will learn fast when war begins, but for now, they are unsure and untried. Much depends on their Warleader.

On this long run for home, I've noted that Midnight matches our pace. She takes her turns with the pack as well, and shares what she has with us. She and that Nosey raccoon are part of the unit we've become. Nosey often spots water first and proves it is good by drinking it. He has twice warned us of bears wandering near our camps. Several times he brought trout from nearby streams and dropped them by the fire—probably after eating some himself, of course. Now we all share dried berries and bannock with him from our own supplies.

I've made a mental note of the streams teeming with trout. It could be a great resource for the People. No one lives in this apparently ignored region between the Grasslands and the River. A rough place, rarely passed through and not really lived in, though garden-like refuges occur where the ground is fairly flat and lush grasses and herbs make a multicolored carpet. Some of the River People families—and the Grassland People as well, according to Midnight—travel to specific places on the River at certain times of the year to gather resources: food, building materials, medicines, and other things. But they missed this area, as we did. This whole new region will help support the People.

I think often about Midnight, even with all of the other things weighing on my mind. Slowly I've come to realize that her strange mannerisms make me smile. She is beautiful and strong, and has contributed greatly to our quest for answers. We were fortunate to find her and gain her detailed knowledge of what is happening, both good and bad, with our enemy of the Spring.

Chapter 8: Midnight Abundance

Far out of my territory for the first time in my life, this land we travel through is astoundingly rich. Coming from the high desert plateau, I'm awed by the lush green plenty we pass through now. This is Fall? I eagerly look forward to the land these men come from. Nosey's gifts of trout are but one taste of the resources all around me. My mother taught me the medicine plants and uses for many other things found in the Grasslands. At home, I might have searched all day, or several days, to find the herbs I want. Here, they grow in abundance everywhere I look! Ordinary edible plants live here as well, and so many plants I don't know.

And the Rivermen! Three more handsome men I have never seen. Serious Boomer, with his huge muscles and lightning reflexes; Seabird's sense of humor, which appears randomly, making me smile even when I tire from the journey, or when I lose myself in sorrow for my People's blindness to what war will mean. Hawk seems to have the best characteristics of the other two, and also that special something that makes him a natural leader.

All three show me courage, honesty, compassion, and respect. A smile blooms within my spirit and I heave a big sigh. None of them have made any romantic suggestions…I catch the daydream in midthought and cast it away…for now. Time enough.

Perhaps.

Chapter 9: Hawk
Last Camp

We travel at a steady pace, not hurrying, although we cover a lot of ground in a day. Landmarks I noted on the way out to the Grasslands become visible: an orphaned boulder at the side of the trail that looks as if some giant dropped it there in passing; a tree split by lightning, healed and growing now with two trunks partway up; a stream cuts the trail, then falls far down a cliff. We are close to Three-Stone Hide. Watching the right side of the trail closely, I finally spot the white stones beside the trail. It's late afternoon and we still have a long run to the village, so I turn off the trail and beckon the others to follow.

"Midnight, I built a hide here and cached a little food…if the crows didn't find it. The hide is too small for five, so you and Nosey can have it and we'll sleep by the fire. Tomorrow you will meet our People."

She smiles at me in a way that I haven't seen before, her eyes soft and warm at the same time, and I abruptly feel my face and ears burn. Flustered, unable to think, I turn to familiar tasks as we set up camp.

Boomer hunts and I work the meadow, gathering fresh greens while Seabird collects firewood. Fall is a good time for roots and tubers since they've had all Summer to plump up with stored starch for the cold season, so I start with them. All I need is a stout pointy stick to dig with and I soon have plenty for our meal.

I hear her voice behind me. "Can you tell me what you are gathering? I don't know many of the plants growing here."

"Of course." I touch a bunch of small spike leaves with the dry remains of globular flowers. "These are onion. They are strong but cook up sweet."

"I know that one, but they are much smaller in the Grasslands. What is this one?"

"Threeleaf. They look nice, but they will kill you."

"Oh! Not this one then."

We share a chuckle and work the meadow together. Midnight learns many new plants and their uses, marveling over the size of those she already knows. She is very pleasant company.

Boomer comes back with three rock rabbits and a pudgy marmot. "Silly thing never saw me! We have fresh meat tonight!" Nosey approaches the pile of game, sniffs it, rises up on hind legs, and his front paws claw at the air as he chitters. It has been a long run on dried meat, berries, the odd trout, and a few other things that Midnight's mother packed.

We foraged all the time we were traveling. About halfway back, Midnight insisted on making a batch of bannock from flour her mother packed for her, and we gnawed on that as we traveled. It's gone now, so Midnight mixes up a small batch from what flour is left and adds some of the onions to the batter, along with some other herbs she found. She cooks them on the hot stones of the firepit where she melted some fat from the marmot.

After we stuff ourselves on the feast, we stretch out around the fire.

"And I thought Copperflower made the best bannock!" I mumble.

Seabird and Boomer grunt agreement. Nosey nuzzles up closer to Midnight.

She laughs. "Wait until I'm used to all these new herbs and roots you have growing around here!"

We decide to forgo the night watches this close to home. A good night's sleep is what we need.

Chapter 10: Midnight
A New Home

I push the hide cover aside and poke my head up. Nosey scrambles out, stopping for a good shake. Bundling the blanket as I crawl out, I replace the layered lid and brush leaves over it and any marks we left climbing in and out. I wander over to the firepit. The sky glows before the sun rises, and as I begin packing, everyone else stirs and rises to the day's tasks. We clean up the camp and do our best to erase our signs, then gather a last time at the trail by the three white stones.

Hawk lays a gentle hand on my arm as I gnaw on a bannock. "Your Shaman brings your people to war against us. You need to think about what that means, if you haven't. You are more than welcome to stay with us, but come the Springtime, we will do whatever it takes to stop them…kill them. You grew up with the warriors who will come. If you like, I will escort you to the Rivergrass People downriver at the Great Water. They are good people and will take you in. You should be safer there as well, since it is a much larger community."

Shocked but pleased at the gesture, I look him straight in the eyes. "First, I do not know any person who would willingly do what they have planned. I thought I knew the People of the Grasslands, and even now I know of some wonderful Grassland People who will have nothing to do with this. Perhaps Shaman cast some spell over the hunters, or perhaps they perceive the chance to become chiefs by stealing land that belongs to others. I can't know for certain, but either way, I have the bond of almost a moon of running trail with you three. I see you to be men of honor, with strength of body, mind, and spirit. I have heard from you all that these things are not acceptable to your tribe. I stand with you and yours against war and slavery."

All three men nod solemnly at my decision, Hawk with a twitch of a smile. Then we step off down the last bit of that long trail.

Chapter 11: Hawk Fishcamp

We push hard on that last run. Even so, it takes most of the day to reach Fishcamp. It's the start of Fall Salmon Time, so nearly everyone comes and goes from their fishing holes and weirs, bringing the catch for their families to clean, smoke, and wind dry the salmon. A few people who have processed their last fish scatter into the bush to gather the last berries or harvest root herbs from the surrounding area. When the salmon run dies out, we all move to Highwater for the Winter. Then the hunters will go after a few more deer before the big rains make it difficult to track them—likely a few weeks away. Perhaps as long as two moons. Our weather is fickle from year to year.

We pass the trail to Highwater and follow the well-beaten and bare trail approach to Fishcamp, stepping onto a planked deck where most people clean and prepare their fish for drying or smoking. The smokehouses belonging to each family are up higher up on the bank so they aren't washed away in a bad flood year. Our homes are even farther up, beyond all but the worst flows in Spring.

Cries of greeting bring more people to welcome us back. Fishcamp is not quite a village, despite the fact we spend almost eight moons of each sun cycle here.

I notice some wide-eyed looks from the younger women and girls who clump together in groups, whispering to each other. Smiling a little, knowing pretty well what is being whispered and wondered, I look at Midnight. She has a little quirk at one corner of her lip and a now-familiar twinkle in her eye as she scans that group. Reaching surreptitiously behind her, I gently touch her arm in reassurance that I stand with her.

We linger in a circle of friends when the crowd parts for Fisheagle, Chief of all the settlements of the River People from Xwèwenaqw east to Chawathil. He wears his regalia: a special blanket woven by the best weavers and a cone-shaped, cedar-strip hat of responsibility, tilted slightly to the right. The affectation reflects his character. He welcomes us briefly, then waves us forward and leads the way up the riverbank to where it tops over and turns to meadow. We follow to his large shed house on the bench of higher ground. Some of the People start after us, but he stops dead, turns brusquely, and holds up one hand.

"I will speak to the travelers alone first. Then we will all gather to share what they have to tell us. Meanwhile, we have lots of work still to be done before Winter!" He smiles to ease any feeling of rebuke and turns away without waiting for a response.

The five of us—six, counting Nosey—follow him into his shed house. The entrance is at ground level, but steps lead down to an excavated floor. Fisheagle sits in his favorite spot on the step ledge that runs all the way around the inside of the structure. He once said to me that he has worn a spot to fit his buttocks, so he always knows where to plant his bottom. We stand in front of him and he gestures to both sides.

"Sit. Take a moment to breathe, then tell me what, and who, you have found." His eyes twinkle at the last.

I lean forward, elbows on knees. "Chief Fisheagle, I present Midnight of the Grassland People. She has proven to be a woman of courage and honor. I offered to take her to the Rivergrass People until any trouble is over, but she has pledged to stay and support us."

The Chief looks into her eyes appraisingly, nods slowly. I know that look from trade negotiations: he accepts what is said but reserves judgment.

"The news is as bad as our worst imagining. The Grassland Shaman readies his warriors to take our territory. He killed—or had killed—the Chief of the Grasslanders and seems to have taken his place. We saw Midnight try to save the Chief, but he died and his house burned. She disrespected the Shaman in front of the whole village."

Fisheagle's eyes harden. "Why?"

"Perhaps you should ask her. She speaks the trade tongue and has already learned some of our words."

The Chief nods.

Midnight rises and moves to stand directly in front of Fisheagle. "Shaman drives the invasion and is likely the one who killed our Chief, a wise and gentle man, surely set against the Shaman's plan. I was fleeing with warning when your men found me."

She paces back and forth in front of him. Nerves, I guess, but you can't tell from her voice.

"Some people of my village will not approve of this war he plans to start, but the Shaman has convinced the hunters to support him, and the war will come." She stops in front of Fisheagle. "I think they will wait until Spring, since it is late in the season. They will use the time to gather young men from all the villages around. It is a serious threat. Drought has ravaged the Grasslands for several years. This hardship drives hunters to become warriors and helps him convince them to go raiding. I believe Shaman's mind is full of worms, or something! He seduces our young people and warriors with tales of plundered food and slaves to do our work." She spreads her hands and shrugs. "The work is our contribution to our People. That is our role. Without that, with slaves doing our work, what does that leave us? The whole idea is foul. If a person does not contribute something real to our community, then they steal from it. The old stories of wars for slaves and territory are ancient, because we learned that it never ends well. Our People die for nothing of permanent value. Certainly nothing to compare with the loss of loved ones and the wisdom of our Elders."

Fisheagle leans back, nods to Midnight. He chews the information with his mind, tasting all the implications.

"Thank you all for learning the truth behind this mystery. I hear and understand what you have said." He shoots a glance at Midnight. "This Shaman, is he mad?"

She nods. "I, and some others, think so. He can fly into a rage at the strangest things. We gave him a place to live when he appeared from the storms of Winter. He has gradually gained more influence over the hunters."

Fisheagle bows his head for a time, and then looks up again. "Yes, I have heard of such a thing. Now I must turn my mind to what we can and will do about it. We have time to think, and to prepare. We must talk to our neighbors as well. We will need allies."

He stands, his shoulders slumped, and heaves a deep sigh. "Go, spend time with your families and friends, and you may tell them what is coming. They will all find out soon enough." He waves us out, muttering, "I foresee fewer of the People this time next year."

As we take our leave, I look back. He paces: head down, brow furrowed.

The four of us gather outside, where the People hunger for news. They swarm around us, concerned because of the Chief's uncharacteristically brusque dismissal earlier. I wait until the rush becomes a trickle and the People are silent, anticipating. The worry on their faces brings the words to me. I summon a loud voice. "We are the River People!"

A rush of sound comes back from the crowd. "We are the River People!"

"Please sit, as in council." The People settle themselves cross-legged on the ground in a deep arc in front and to the sides. I remain standing so I can turn to any speaker.

"The Grassland People bring war to us next Spring." A hiss, mingled with growls, arises.

"They would take our land for themselves. They wish to kill and enslave our People to expand their territory."

Now it's a susurration of anger tinged with threat.

"The Grassland Shaman wants what we built through hard work so he and his warriors can live in comfort in our stolen homes. They wish for all that is ours. They desire our loved ones—men, women and children—as slaves; they seek to live in comfort in your homes, eating food you gather for them."

The crowd begins to heave like waves in a storm. Redwolf, known for his short temper, stands and shouts, "Then they will die!"

I hold up a hand to him. "We are not going to war! If they bring it to us, we will defeat them. We are known for our balance of wisdom and courage. We will find the right path. War is the final answer, when all other choices lie dead before us. But one of theirs discovered this plan and had the honor and the courage to bring it to us!"

I sweep my arm toward Midnight, who rises to stand next to me, tall and proud. Nosey sits at her feet, jutting his toothy face up at the crowd in challenge as she stands and plants her staff, solidly anchored in River earth, connecting her to the land as she stands before them. The crowd roars their approval and I know she enters their hearts in that moment. She is family.

"River People, we have things to do! The Chief has heard our story and he already plans the strategy, so go to your tasks. That food will give us strength to stop them. We work for our lives now—our freedom, our families, our People!"

***

The crowd breaks up and the People disperse. Some groups of hunters gather in a group, fire flickering in their eyes. Turning away, I come face-to-face with Midnight. She gently seizes my head and pulls our lips together. I lose myself for a moment as I surrender to the joy of it.

"Mine," she whispers. I realize I haven't taken a breath for some time. Taking a much-needed gasping gulp of air, I wonder, *Is there a trick to it? Perhaps I need more practice.* A glow grows in the core of my mind, body, and spirit. It rushes with the hot blood in my veins. A change that I can't describe goes to the center of who I am and what I want. Right now, I want more practice kissing…

I lead Midnight to my family's house. My mother, Smallwave, will be cleaning and sorting roots for storage. My father probably fishes on the River. He wasn't at the gathering, so he is likely at the family fish weir, a way downriver from Fishcamp. My mother looks up as I brush aside the blanket that covers the entry to our shed house and she runs to wrap her arms around me.

"Where have you been? Oh!" She stops cold as Midnight straightens behind me.

"Ten, this is Midnight. I, uh, found her on my journey. She has that effect on me as well." I call my mother "Ten"—our affectionate family word for "Mother."

"Whoop! You've done well while away! First I hear you saved us all from slavery, or worse—some of the other mothers stopped by to tell me—and now this!"

She kisses me on the cheek and holds me tight for a moment. Her expression shifts to a familiar concerned scowl. "Are you all right? All parts accounted for?"

She steps back and looks me over, one eyebrow cocked, mouth tight, hands on her hips. "You're skinny."

I chuckle. "I suppose. I believe I have all the parts I left with. Tired from a very long journey, but good."

She nods, seeming satisfied with her inspection, and pushes me away.

"Fine. I will hear all about your adventure later. Perhaps Midnight will fill me in. Then you can tell the tale to your father when he returns from the fishing hole. Drop your weapons and gear, then go away for a little while, son. We women need to talk."

My younger sister Freebird stands beside Midnight and takes her hand with a gentle smile.

Ten nods. "Children can sense character. She still might be trouble, but it would be a good kind. No, don't worry. You have proved your wisdom. She is safe with me, and tonight we will hear all about your adventures. Now it's women time. Go, whish. Go out."

She pushes me away toward the doorway. I look at Midnight, unsure… She smiles a little nervously back at me, then nods.

So, I go. I learned a long time ago that arguing with my mother is a really bad idea. I look longingly one last time at Midnight as I duck the door blanket on the way out. Outside, I take a deep breath and blow it out in a great *whoosh*. That definitely didn't go as I expected. I know I will find out what my immediate future is going to be like when the women tell me. It's their way. I have spoken with several two-spirit friends, both male and female couples, who say that it is the same with them. Perhaps it is an occasional role that must be filled in any good relationship. Regardless, I have been dismissed. I shrug my shoulders and go look for Seabird and Boomer.

My progress is very slow. Everyone thanks me for warning the People. Some of the men congratulate me for finding such a woman. Some of the women, all young and single—including one Copperflower of the delicious bannock—greet me very warmly. I detect a hint of something different in some of their eyes. Not really understanding and with my face burning from the attention, I work my way toward Boomer's house, seeking male companionship and his home being closest. I spot him talking to his father, named Sharpstick because, as a young hunter, he once ran a bear off a kill with a sharp stick. When I come up to them, Sharpstick grasps my arms.

"Thank you, Hawk. You brought my son home safe."

I smile and return the greeting. "I think it was the other way around."

Boomer snorts. "You saw what the blazes might mean and led us into enemy territory. We got the story, and you got us all back safe. Then you tell the village what is coming and rile them up 0to be ready for it. And you caught the girl! When the war comes, I want to be right next to you."

Seabird walks up in time to hear Boomer's reply. "Me too!"

I grasp an arm of each of them. "We—all of us—will win this war. We have to."

I spend the rest of the afternoon and evening wandering with Boomer and Seabird, answering questions from other villagers about our journey and what we need to do to prepare for the Spring invasion. As is always the case, the young are more than ready to fight, in their own minds. The older ones, some of whom have experienced much smaller scale raids, are determined but much less eager. Boomer, who has fought in a couple of opportunistic raids in the past, notes, "The youngsters will have the piss knocked out of them in the first battle. Then we'll find out who is steady and who will be running supplies."

Finally, the worried questions we often have no good answers for taper off. It is late and we split up, each headed to our homes. As I come close, my stomach muscles tighten. Midnight and Ten have had a lot of time together. *What did they discuss?* I wonder…

I reach the house and inside I find my father, Ten, my younger sister Freebird, Midnight, and Nosey. They are all focused on me with some intense purpose in their eyes. My face flushes red-hot as my imagination runs wild. Nosey appears to grin, displaying all of his needle-like teeth, and the rest of them burst into laughter. Not what I expected.

My father clears his throat. "Sit down, son." I slide awkwardly into a spot on the bench. Midnight, Nosey following, slips onto the bench next to me. She takes my arm and holds it tight as Nosey snuggles up on my other side. He's never done that before.

Ten lays a reassuring hand on my arm. "I suppose we've tormented you enough. I had a word with the Chief. I have an unused storage hut among the trees behind his house. Do you know it?" I nod.

Ten smiles. "You three have the use of it until we move to Highwater. We will figure out what to do for permanent housing later. We have set it all up for you and it should be quite comfortable, and private." Her practical face brightens with a delighted and mischievous grin. "You have no idea how happy you have made your father and me. We were starting to worry about the shortage of grandchildren in the house! It is so quiet in here when you are out hunting, your dad is fishing, and Freebird is off with her friends."

I look around at similar gleeful expressions on everyone's faces, except, perhaps, Nosey. I can't really tell what the raccoon's face is saying, but it involves many sharp white fangs and he's pawing the air in my direction, so I figure it is about the same as everyone else.

"First you will eat here with us. I tell you, I quite like this girl who found you. She pitched in and helped set everything up at the hut, then dove in and helped with dinner. I look forward to tasting her fry bread. She put things in it that I have never tried, but it smells delicious!"

I sniff and finally notice that it does smell wonderful in the house.

"Thank you, all. I had no idea what we were going to do for any of that. Boomer, Seabird, and I answered questions for the People all afternoon. I didn't think about this."

"We know," my father says. "We each have roles to fulfill. You are becoming a leader. I provide for my growing family, as does your mother. Your sister is still learning her responsibilities and exploring her options."

I dart a suspicious glance at my sister and see another one of those toothy grins. Nosey has already had an impact on my family. I glance at Ten, who seems happily content.

She nods. "Midnight is also discovering and choosing her way. She is quite the young woman, and we could not be happier with her choice."

I blink at that, look at Midnight, and notice she is as flushed as I felt earlier.

Freebird interjects, impatiently. "Let's eat!"

Chapter 12: Hawk
The Song

After the supper, Midnight and I walk up the bank to the hut, arms gentle around each other. Nosey waddles behind. The whole family has spoiled him with treats and bits. *Family…* My life is changing.

***

Morning breaks, very brightly, and I drift through the village in a daze. One faint part of my mind registers that everyone is smiling at me today. I sort of notice, but my mind and heart are reliving the moments of the night: the feel of her, the bond building between us, the sharing.

I have been intimate with women in the past, but last night was a revelation of what that can be. I don't have the words to describe the experience fully. We joined in more than bodies—our spirits soared together, hearts pounding as one. We caressed each other; we played like children with a new game. The night was too short, but we finally lay exhausted, entwined still as dawn began to light the sky as though it too celebrated our union.

Midnight fell asleep, but I could not, so I dressed and walked the village as the sun rose above the horizon.

I remember seeing the two-spirit couple this morning, Redwolf and Sandwalker. I focused a little better when Redwolf punched my arm hard enough that it penetrated my happy, bewildered fog.

"Hawk! You finally did it! You found someone who loves your admittedly handsome but vaguely officious self!"

Sandwalker slapped me on the back so hard that my body snapped forward and my head didn't quite keep up.

"And such a magnificent mate! I expected you to settle in with some comfortably built girl with great cooking skills. I didn't think you would ever manage such a woman as Midnight. Well done, lad! But hang on tight. I have a feeling you are tied to a thunderstorm."

I think I wandered off again after that.

***

Sometime later, Seabird runs up. "Hey, if you can shake yourself out of it, I have something to tell you that requires your full attention."

I stop. My brain partly recognizes this might be important. I summon a full body shake that helps me to concentrate. "What?"

"Good, you're back. You had me worried for a minute." Seabird wears the same wicked grin I vaguely remember seeing on several family members' faces the night before. Even the raccoon's.

"A runner from the Rivergrass People arrived. We gave her our news and she gave us some back."

I start to fade again into the river of bliss. Seabird snaps his fingers a couple of times in front of my eyes. "Focus!"

With great effort, I obey. "Sorry—I didn't sleep."

"Yes, I know the woman and it truly surprises me that you're up and walking this morning. You must be tougher than I thought."

I clear my throat. "Ok, what's the news?"

"A giant canoe pulled into the bay at Rivergrass Village yesterday. It has huge sheets of something on poles to catch the wind. They have come to trade, but not the usual trade goods between the People. They are willing to trade knowledge of how to make things we've never seen, including weapons!"

Fully attentive now, the memories of the night fade into the back of my mind, but a strong ember of the fire remains deep inside.

"I have to talk to them."

"That's better! Let's find Boomer and go."

"I have a better idea. Collect Boomer, the Chief, and about six solid rowers. We'll take a canoe."

"Done! The messenger can row as well and we'll give her a ride home." Seabird nods and sprints away.

I turn back and run to the hut where Midnight still sleeps inside. An instant stirring distracts me. I struggle and tamp it down because I know she will want to go with me.

I shake her gently. Her eyes open, alert and mischievous, and she grins with smoky wisps of last night's fire in her eyes. The passion flares again, but duty calls.

"Grab your weapons—and Nosey, of course—and meet me at the canoes down at Fishcamp. Anyone can send you the right way. A trader arrived at Rivergrass with things to trade that we've never seen before. He comes from the Great Water beyond the Big Island, and I have to tell the Chief."

Midnight's eyes narrow as she sloughs off both the blanket and the vestiges of our night. "I'll meet you."

I lean in for one more taste of her, and then run off to the Chief's house, conveniently close by. I find Fisheagle still at breakfast and tell him what I know. Sharp as always, he nods.

"Have you got a crew?"

"Seabird is preparing everything. Will you join us?"

"I have to grab a couple of things, and then I'll meet you at Fishcamp."

***

We steer the canoe onto the big beach at Rivergrass Village. A group comes toward us. Fisheagle, now wearing his full regalia, leaps onto the long beach first from his place in the bow of the canoe, one hand holding his hat as his blanket flares around. I follow right behind.

I adopt my trading face: interested but wary. Scanning the crowd, I focus on a wholly strange-looking man with the Rivergrass group. His unusual eyes fold slightly at the outside corners and his skin is the color of freshly carved yellow cedar. His hair, dark like ours but gathered into a very long braid, wraps around his neck and hangs down his front. A translucent greenstone confines and weighs down the tail end. His ornate and shimmery robe is covered with strange animals and patterns, beautifully sewn. Its many colors glisten in the sunlight like fish oil on water.

The Rivergrass Chief, Kiapelaneh, very dignified in his regalia, welcomes us formally to his territory. He turns to Fisheagle and both men grasp the other's forearm as they speak the traditional words of greeting. I stay close enough to hear clearly as Kiapelaneh presents Fisheagle to the stranger.

"Zahn, I present Fisheagle, Chief of the River People. Fisheagle, Zhan is of the Song People. He comes to trade from the west, across the Great Water beyond the Big Island."

Zahn puts his hands together and bows gracefully to Chief Fisheagle and his companions: legs straight, he bends at the waist, then returns erect and says, "Me not speak well." He struggles to say that in the trade tongue, and he keeps moving his hands as though trying to shape the words.

He turns and waves to a tall man in the crowd. A Haida, also in full regalia, walks toward us. His blanket signifies he is both Sea Hunter and Warrior. He smiles, hands empty and open.

Speaking the trade tongue with a northern accent, he addresses us.

"Greetings from my Haida People. My name is Ts'aak: warrior, whale killer, sea-master, trader. I have traded down this way a few times in the past. The Song visited us twice before and offer many useful things to trade. I will try to speak for Trader Zahn during his first journey this far south. We have not mastered their language."

Fisheagle steps straight in, right to business. "We welcome Ts'aak of the Haida and Zahn of the Song. What does he seek to trade for, and what does he offer?"

Zahn beams broadly as Ts'aak translates. The trader bows to Fisheagle and speaks slowly to Ts'aak for a short time.

Ts'aak turns to the River People. "Zahn speaks: 'You have many beautiful fur animals that do not live where we come from. Also, you have the red metal...'" Zahn reaches out and touches Fisheagle's arm where he has a finely worked copper band. "He offers knowledge of how to make fire powder. It has many uses—one is to help mine the red metal. The powder can also be used as a weapon to defeat your enemies. He will teach you this secret in exchange for an agreed-upon number of good fur pelts and an amount of the red metal. You may also suggest any other items for his inspection that you think he may be interested in."

Fisheagle lowers his eyes for a moment of private thought, then raises his head and waves an open hand to Zahn as he says to Ts'aak, "This fire powder is interesting. I would appreciate a demonstration. Indeed, we have many beautiful pelts, and will have even more after the Winter. I also think that we can supply the red metal in quantities he will appreciate. It will take some time to collect from the rock it lives in, although you say that this fire powder may help with it."

Ts'aak turns to Zahn and speaks. Zahn listens intently and smiles again at the end. He addresses Ts'aak for a minute, then turns and signals to his people farther up the beach.

A volley of about twenty arrows arcs out over the water, spitting sparks and black smoke until they splash into the water with a hiss of steam. An archer steps forward with a stout, double recurved bow and an arrow wrapped in what looks like soiled cloth behind the head. He passes the arrowhead through the fire. It begins to throw sparks and he swings it toward a wooden post sunk in the sand. He pulls, holds it a second, then releases. It strikes the post and burns for a short time until the post catches fire, and soon blazes like a giant torch.

Zahn stretches out a hand toward a rock, about the size of a full-grown bear. A dirty-looking piece of string hangs from a small hole that looks to have been chipped into a crack. Another small fire burns nearby and one of the Song pulls a burning twig from it, walks over to the rock, and holds the fire to the string. It spits bright sparks in all directions, like the arrows did, and the Song sailor turns and runs like a bear is chasing him. A thunderous blast shatters the rock and small bits of and chips patter like hail onto the sand in a large circle around where the stone used to be amid a cloud of smoke and dust.

Our People from both villages recover from the shock. Some of the closest shake their heads and hold their ears. Fisheagle dusts his regalia off as he walks up to Zahn and Ts'aak.

"Let's talk."

Kiapelaneh gestures agreement with a flourish of his open hand. Zahn smiles again, signals to one of his crew, and the man runs to a small boat on the shore and returns with a padded stool that sinks to its cross-braces in the dry sand as Zahn sits. Ts'aak stands next to him, ready to translate, and the onlooking locals close in around them to listen.

"Fire powder is three parts: one is coal, a black stone that lives in the ground, or charcoal, which is made by burning wood in a special way so it doesn't all turn to ash. We make large piles of tightly stacked wood that hold the heat in and use wet blankets to keep air out as it burns. The second part is a bright yellow stone that is soft, easy to make into powder. You have such a stone?"

I recall seeing something similar. "It turns the earth yellow and smells very bad after a fire has been near it?"

Zahn nods. "That is right."

Midnight speaks up. "We have pockets of it in the Grasslands, usually near the base of hills, or in rocky places."

"So, you have the second part." Zahn smiles and inclines his head. "The third part is powder made by a complicated and slow process from large amounts of old urine. I will bring the powder to you to trade."

Fisheagle and Kiapelaneh look at each other. As one they sign AGREEMENT and Ts'aak nods, relaying their affirmative response.

"I have decided to lend you four of my sailors who know these things and will teach you. Two will stay here, and the other two will go your territory." He fixes his eyes on Fisheagle. "Your land is upriver from here?"

Fisheagle nods as he hears the translation. He scans the beach and selects a twig the length of his forearm. He begins to sketch a line map in the dry sand. His rendition is excellent, showing the major islands and the twists and turns of the channel from where we are, the delta, to the northward turn where the River emerges from the mountains east of Highwater.

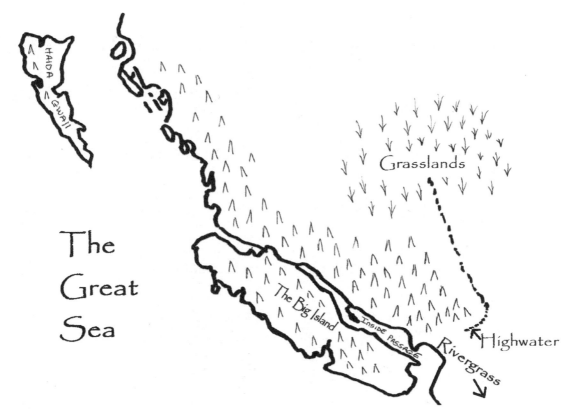

The Great Sea

He looks up at Zahn, who is bent over intently. "Here we are now. Our village on the River is here, and our winter village is on higher ground, here. We have frequent floods in both Spring and Fall. Our Winters vary. Some are mild; others bring blizzards and deep snowdrifts, particularly when an outflow of freezing air funnels down into the wet valley from the interior." Fisheagle stops a moment to let Ts'aak catch up.

"I would not recommend bringing your vessel upriver, as the sand and gravel bars move around constantly. Our canoes give us the ability to negotiate the route, and we have large cargo canoes for transporting goods."

Zahn smiles. "You have an excellent grasp of what we need to manage our trade. I am happy to share this knowledge with you. The advisors I leave behind will learn your language. Ours has many words, like the number of the stars in the sky! But having a common tongue will make us better trade partners, good for both."

Zahn pauses for the translation to finish, Ts'aak clearly struggling to keep up.

"I'm interested in animal pelts that have been fixed for the sea voyage so they don't rot—I see you have the skill. I'm also looking for a greenstone. Do you have it? The advisors know it if they see it. They will also teach you how to make the red metal run like water from the stone it lives in so I can carry more on the ship. It's a very long journey from my home to here. I will not try the passage in Winter, so make two, perhaps three voyages in a year. Hmm—these carvings. Can your carvers make small objects for trade?"

Kiapelaneh stands. "I will speak to the carvers. They may have some art they would part with."

He sweeps his arm to the west. "The sun falls to his rest and food will be ready. We should go to the lodge to feast with our visitors. We can continue our talks with food."

Once inside, I sit with Kiapelaneh and Fisheagle. Next to us, Midnight is beside Ts'aak, and Zahn, who seems very relaxed, but I sense his calm posture does not entirely show the truth. Talk revolves around two topics: trade items and the threat from the east.

Kiapelaneh leans over to Ts'aak. "Your people make alliances with your neighbors. I understand your culture allows for limited warfare to gain resources: food, copper, even territory."

"It is true. The spirits give us strength and courage to fight our enemies. Sometimes those are not enough and we lose. Other times we are tired of fighting. In these times, we ally with our neighbors, and together we are much too formidable to attack. Those are times of peace. We harvest the bounty of the waters and the land and grow fat and happy, and make many babies!" His belly laugh fills the hall, garnering more than a few smiles.

I speak up. "So, alliance brings peace and prosperity to the peoples?"

He hesitates. "Yes, it is true. But then someone always manages to do something foolish, which breaks the alliance. Then we fight again."

"Alliances can't last?"

"I suppose they could, if we could keep the hotheads from being stupid, but that's the problem. Even good people, smart people, eventually do something reckless to someone else and we have war."

I nod thanks to him and catch Fisheagle and Kiapelaneh looking at me with surprise. Fisheagle moves closer and whispers, "You are wiser even than I gave you credit for. Stay with us for the evening. You are on the same trail as we are."

Chapter 13: Midnight Genesis

The morning after the feast, I awake early to the aroma of fry bread. We slept in the hall with the rest of our party. I jump up and help prepare breakfast: bannock with berries baked in. We also make thin strips of venison toasted on the fire. I like to nibble on the venison strips after a few bites of bannock. The cooks are very kind to Nosey, dropping bits on the floor.

Zahn and his people retired to their ship for the night, but as the sun rises and paints the clouds with pinks and orange, Zahn enters the longhouse with Ts'aak and four of his sailors. They bow to me in passing, and I bow the same short bow back. I rather like the custom. Whether it's truly meant or simply a custom, it is a sign of respect.

***

After the meal, Zahn invites the chiefs aboard his ship for a tour. Hawk and I decide to tag along. Zahn doesn't object, even with Nosey following behind.

The vessel is shaped like a low topped moccasin: lower in the bow, slightly closer to the water in the waist, and tall and proud at the back. Ts'aak explains the steering oar is below and behind the stern. Ropes run up to a mechanism for the steersman. Five scraped tree trunks support the ship, with slanted poles that give structure to the wind-catchers. Those resemble cedar-bark fans we make for the heat of Summer, or when a blizzard's cold pushes smoke down into the home. The wind-catchers are heavy woven cloth attached to the crosspieces. Ts'aak says that the structure allows Zahn to raise and lower the cloth panels and move them around to catch the wind better, or to catch less wind. At the stern, two beams stick out to support a wide canoe with a squared back end, lashed up tight against the beams to keep it from swinging in rough water.

The front of the boat ends in a wide, flat platform over a sharply pointed nose, where Nosey is currently exploring. He's sniffing at every object on deck. I keep one eye on him so he doesn't catch the scent of something tasty and go below into the vessel.

Parallel strips of wood attach to the sides of the boat to make the hull. They run from nose to tail, each board lapped on top of the one below, leaving an exposed ridge the thickness of the overlapping board. Ts'aak tells me the ridges help to keep it from rolling in rough water. Taken as a whole, it is a highly functional piece of art.

Hawk draws my attention to several frames on the deck that support a smooth round piece of wood, like a short log, with metal straps holding it to a frame anchored to the deck. Ropes run from the masts to these structures. Where the ends of the log stick out on both ends of the frame, holes are drilled into the log and stout sticks inserted. Seen end on, they look like a sun with rays. Hawk asks Ts'aak about them, and he explains that they allow a few men to raise and lower the large wind-catchers easily by winding the ropes around the log or loosening them off. The sticks give the device leverage. I file it as a useful idea and look around for other interesting concepts.

The way pieces of wood are fastened together intrigues me. Much of the construction is perfectly drilled and pegged, and I ask Ts'aak how they drill the wood so perfectly. He has to confer with Zahn, who calls to one of the Song sailors. He brings a long piece of metal attached to a crosspiece handle. The metal rod has spiral grooves cut into it, further sharpened to a knife edge all along the groove.

The sailor demonstrates on a piece of scrap wood he brought with him—the rod cuts cleanly into the wood. Amazingly, in moments, the tool bores a perfect hole. I have not seen any here, on the coast, but back in the Grasslands, friendly wood bees the spirits send make perfect holes like this.

I thank him and Zahn with a little bow and ask Ts'aak if that is something the Song could bring in trade next time. Ts'aak confers with Zahn for a few moments and the trader smiles.

"Zahn says you are very wise, and he will return with a variety of tools to trade."

Zahn converses with Ts'aak some more. "The Song must prepare to depart. Zahn says he looks forward to a return voyage in the Springtime."

Ts'aak hesitates as he chooses his words. "As for me, I will speak to our People about your proposal of Alliance. If the chiefs think it is wise, I may be back soon, depending on the weather. In the meantime, take care, and know that I enjoyed our time together. Zahn's advisors will teach you many things and will learn your trade language. They are chosen for their skills. Treat them well, for they are priceless gifts."

The chiefs grasp arms with Ts'aak in farewell as Zahn waves to one of his crew over and speaks briefly. He also beckons the sailor with the auger, takes the tool, and nods. The other sailor returns from the bowels of the vessel bearing two gray metal axes with wooden handles. He presents one axe to each of the chiefs and, bowing, hands the hole-making tool to me.

Unable to express my thanks, I turn to Ts'aak. "Please tell Zahn that he honors us with his gifts."

Ts'aak listens to Zahn for a moment, then turns back to me. "Zahn is pleased that you recognize its value. He warns that the gray metal hates water and will turn red and begin to crumble if it's left wet. Clean and dry it after use, and perhaps rub it with some old fat to keep water from harming it. That works for us."

I bow again to Zahn and Ts'aak and turn to the walkway leading to shore, scooping up Nosey. When we are all off the ship, I watch the crew lift the ramp using one of their rope-winding devices and a swing pole. They use another of the devices at the front of the ship to lift a large stone out of the ocean. The stone has a hole in the center that the rope is tied to and they lower it carefully into a sturdy box fixed to the deck.

The ship turns slowly away from the shore until it faces northwest. The sailors scramble among the ropes and panels, adjusting and pulling here and there. Then the great vessel leaps up a southbound wave and begins cutting the water, headed north again.

It is a magnificent sight.

***

Now that the trader has gone, we can digest all we've seen and heard.

Kiapelaneh suggests an alliance between Rivergrass and the River People. "We will share in the trade with the Song. We know that you must prepare for war in the Springtime, so we pledge food—as much as we can provide without starving our own. We will still hunt and fish. Preserving can be done even when the weather turns. I firmly believe the Grasslanders are taken by greed. They will see us as the next victims if they conquer you. You are the River, but we are kin, as the River and the Sea. They *must* be stopped."

Fisheagle decides to stay at Rivergrass with one canoe and four rowers. The rest of us load up and begin the journey upstream to home.

Chapter 14: Hawk Highwater

As soon as we return to Fishcamp, I call the River folk together again at the village center. Almost all, except some hunters, are here processing salmon, steelhead, and trout for the long Winter. Berries and other fruits are already dried for storage, as are some herbs.

"Fisheagle tasked us to prepare Highwater and I will lead some of you to start work on fortifications. You certainly don't need me to tell you how to process fish!"

I wait for the merriment to die off and continue. "That location is the better choice to defend because of the River and our hilltop. Fishcamp is right at the water, which leaves us no line of retreat away from inland invaders. Highwater has the northern stone wall that rises behind, giving us sight and fire zones for half a circle, and more in front. I don't believe they know the trails to the top. Our scouts found no blazes or other sign on them.

"With log walls and raised walkways—an idea passed on by one of the Song advisors—we will have even more advantage of height to fire down on the invaders' troops, as they will be confined to a fairly narrow strip of land and the meadows. New lifting technology that we noted on the Song ship will make construction much faster and easier.

"I will lead the advance party to Highwater while the rest of us finish in the salmon fishery and preserve the catch. My group's first tasks are to plan the fortifications, dig ditches around the hilltop, and start falling trees. Two Song advisors from across the Western Sea are here to learn our language and show us better ways to do certain things. Their names are Zizhan and Wei. One will stay with you here at Fishcamp to help and learn our ways, and the other will come to Highwater with me to advise on construction. Make them welcome as best you can. They know little of our language, but they have been ordered to learn. Meanwhile, we will use hand sign language for basic communication."

Highwater is our winter village, and it is very different from Fishcamp. Instead of sheds and a few pit houses on higher ground above the River, Highwater is a collection of cedar-planked and -pole frame houses clustered around a huge central lodge atop a wooded plateau. Our stories tell us that it has been defensible in the far past, but those were against a few smaller raids than the one we now face.

First thing, I guide Midnight to our family's Highwater house, where she gratefully sheds her pack. Highwater is our late Fall, Winter, and early Spring home, when the River is often flooding over its banks. Fishcamp's facilities are strictly for our long fishing season, lasting from mid-Spring—whenever the River flow calms—to mid- or late-Fall, depending on the River's mood each year.

We drop our gear, and then I take Zizhan, the Song advisor, to a guesthouse on the perimeter of the village. Zizhan seems very thankful—honored, even. He bows repeatedly to me, which makes me…uncomfortable. I don't understand why a house is such an honor, since the village has several available to travelers and traders. I hope Zizhan and the other Song man learn our language quickly, as I have many questions.

The work party settles into their winter homes. At midday, we gather in the space in front of the big lodge where Zizhan signs that he wants to tour the perimeter of the hilltop. Midnight and I walk with him to the edge of the plateau and around the perimeter. When we return to our starting point, he bends to the ground and begins to trace designs in the dirt. Many of the People gather to see what we are doing.

Zizhan draws the long oval shape of the plateau top. He sketches a square inside and marks the outlines of the existing buildings pretty accurately. He draws another square between the buildings and the first line, then points to the outer line and makes digging motions, tracing the line deeper and wider.

He walks to a tree and taps it with a stick. He makes motions of chopping down the tree, then, holding his hands in front of him, makes up and down motions with both hands as he rotates in a circle. Then he goes back to his diagram in the dirt and uses his stick to make a line of little circles going around the inside line.

Patting a tree, I point to the inside line, then point to the outside line and make digging motions. Zizhan leaps up, smiles broadly, and nods agreement before bowing to me again.

I call a couple of older hunters over. "See if you can kill a deer or two, and anything else you come across. We need good food for this crew and the work ahead." They leave at a trot and I turn to Midnight. "Would you take charge of the lodge? We will gather there for rests and meals. I've got to keep the workers fed and strong to finish in time."

She grabs me for a kiss and it stops my world for a moment. She skips off while I still feel paralyzed. I shake myself, straighten up and growl, "Let's have it done then!" The people go off to find tools and Zizhan is smiling about something.

We settle into a routine. I set half of the men to dig the perimeter trench, and the other half are tasked with falling and limbing trees for the inner wall. It soon becomes clear that we will need to bring more logs up from below. I sit with Zizhan one evening and communicate to him that we should build winches like I saw on the ship. He nods and indicates he will build them, but he wants one man to help. I agree and ask Woodshaper, a carver, to help him.

With that in the works, I bend my mind to weapons. The main weapon for the River People is the bow. All of the men, and most of the women, carry them. What we will need is a lot of arrows. Those are time consuming to make and take some skill to shape properly. We must find shafts of the right size—of strong wood that will dry straight—and then heads are next on my list. Those have to be carefully chipped from hard flintstone, or from the greenstone that got Zizhan very excited when he saw it. He called it "*Yumi Yu*" and says that Zahn will give very good trade for it. I make a mental note to bring some to the next trade session with the Song. Also, feathers will be collected for arrow fletching. *I wish the rest of the People would finish with the fish and come to Highwater to help with all the tasks that need doing.*

I decide some warclubs should be made for close quarters fighting, if it comes to that. Better to have them and not need them than to need them and not have them. I also consider lining the raised walkways we will build with head-sized stones we could throw down on attackers. I stop myself. *We don't even have a wall yet!*

Zizhan learns words quickly, but real conversation is still difficult and mostly done with gestures and pictures drawn in the dirt. I decide to try to ask him about weapons.

I find him and the carver called Maskmaker cutting rounds from the long trunk of a bigleaf maple. They have hatchets and are each working on opposite sides of the log. When they get too deep in one wedge and the hatchets begin to get stuck, they rotate the trunk, cutting the next section deeper.

I call both of them away and kneel in the dirt. They squat next to me as I first draw a bow and arrow, then a warclub. I point to Zizhan and spread my hands and look questioningly at him, shrugging my shoulders. Zizhan examines my crude drawings. Then he points to the bow, arrow, and spear and makes motioning gestures toward himself. I jump up and run to where my weapons are, nearby, and bring them to him.

Zizhan looks them over carefully, seemingly lost in thought for a few minutes, sometimes shaking his head. He rises to his feet and paces back and forth. At one point, he even slaps both sides of his head, as if to knock something loose. Finally, he kneels and draws a stout handle with a double-pointed crosspiece at one end: a double-ended spike on a handle. Then he draws another handle. This one has a ball on the end. He looks around and finds a roundish rock, which he places at the end of the drawn handle. He mimes wrapping something around the stone and handle.

I nod understanding. Some of the People carry warclubs, but both new designs look like vicious hand-to-hand weapons. I bow thanks to Zizhan, then point at the tree they were working on. He stands and walks away.

I know the Song make better weapons, but they use the gray hard metal. The copper my People know how to work is too soft for weapons, although… A thought comes and I stop still to think it through.

If we could make the copper into sharp arrowheads, it might take less time than to fashion the stone heads we use now. Driven by a bow, they would cut flesh. I tuck that away for the moment. I want to talk to the copper artists who make the arm and wrist bands the People wear. We never used copper for weapons, and we will need the copper for trade with the Song.

I walk up to one of the diggers working on the trench. "Coyote, run back to Fishcamp and find a copper worker. Bring him or her back as soon as you can."

Coyote grins. "I was ready for a break anyway." He drops his digging stick and heads out.

I pick the stick up out of the trench and fall to work, spiking it into the dry earth and pulling it back to break the soil. Spike, pull, spike, pull, spike, pull…

Behind the breakers come the scoopers with wooden shovels. Some use bare hands to toss the clods out. The center of Highwater is trampled regularly by foot traffic, but the diggers are near the edge of the flat hilltop on two sides, so mostly it isn't packed too hard. Three breakers work side by side, a bit more than an arm's reach apart. The top of the trench will be about a body length wide and will taper a bit to provide good cover about waist deep for the archers. Any deeper and they would struggle to climb out for a charge. Crouched down, they'd be out of sight, even moving, able to pop up randomly to shoot into the enemy.

I also plan on retreat channels leading back under the wall on the two sides close to the drop-off, with large stones nearby that can be rolled to block the channels from inside. We will keep stakes at each channel that can be quickly driven into the ground to stop the boulders from being pushed back in an attack.

***

We make good progress for the rest of the next two days. Then Coyote shows up with three women and five more men. I send them to work on the trench but one of the women, named Sunshine, is a coppersmith who makes armbands, bracelets, and ear dangles. I take her aside and speak to her about my idea for copper arrowheads.

She thinks for a while. "I normally shape the metal that has been beaten into sheets. What you need is to melt the copper and pour it into molds, which takes a very hot fire and special techniques, but we know a very soft gray metal that might work. Let me think on this for a while."

I nod agreement. "You might talk to the Song advisor here, his name is Zizhan. I will bring him to you."

I introduce them, and then try to explain what is in my mind to Zizhan. The Song man is puzzled for a long time, trying to figure out what we want. Finally, he stops us and carefully asks, with signs and a couple of words, "What, exactly, do you want to do?"

I bend down and draw a sketch of an arrowhead. Then I draw one of my arrows and show it to Zizhan. I try several ways to explain the problem. Finally, Zizhan smiles and nods. He gestures to wait, then runs off. Sunshine and I talk about the problem for a while, but it is clear that we don't possess the knowledge to do what is in my mind, which is to mold metal quickly into arrowheads.

Some while later, Zizhan returns with a bowl filled with what looks like River clay, fine grained and sticky, and two scraps of plank he scrounged up. He pulls out his knife and starts carving the shape of an arrowhead into one of the planks. When he is done, he presses the clay into the mold and scrapes off the excess. He ties the other plank over the first, then shoves the whole thing under the dirt and ashes next to the fire. He points to the sun and mimes its movement for some time, then goes back to working on the winches.

Sunshine laughs.

"What?"

"He's making pottery arrowheads!"

"Of course! That solves our problem with the metal and the stone. We make a lot of molds, and we can make arrowheads as fast as we can make the shafts!"

"You don't need a metal worker, you need potters." Sunshine smiles at me. "I carve pretty well, good enough for this. I'll help you make the molds, or I can go back and send you some other people who can do what you need."

I sit silent for a bit while I think about the new process. "If you could start, it would be appreciated. We may need to test some firing methods and shapes and sizes. With your help, we will be days ahead. I can't shake this feeling that we need to be ready sooner, rather than later."

Sunshine nods and leaves in search of materials. I go looking for a potter and ask among all the people who have come, but none are potters. Disappointed, I go back to digging the trench.

Spike, pull, spike, pull, spike, pull…

Chapter 15: Hawk
Rats in the Meadow

Over the next few days, more people from Fishcamp start trickling in. The salmon run has died off, quite literally. No one is very interested in spawned-out fish lying dead and rotting in the sun on the gravel beaches and bars, except the carrion eaters: eagles, bears, coyotes, crows, seagulls, raccoons, and the bugs.

We caught and processed a good amount of food over the season. The River People never take more than they need for a hard Winter because the animals need to fatten up. They know that Winter can be long, and it is always hard to find food before the Spring awakening and the early run of salmon.

I meet each group of new arrivals, looking for potters. Finally I find one, named Clayshaper, of course. I ask him to see me when he is settled into his winter home.

The fighting trench is almost complete, with some deepening still needed in places. It extends all around the top of Highwater's plateau and I've already started pulling diggers off that task to help set logs in the palisade. They'll be about twice the length of a man behind the trench. The treecutters made a good pile of logs, and the wall starts to take shape.

A nagging feeling nibbles at my concentration, whispering that time is running out. Slowly it grows stronger, pushing me to drive the workers. I have no conscious reason to worry, and that bothers me even more. I decide to send out a scout party. I choose six hunters and send them as three pairs, with instructions to separate and search along the trail. They are to observe the enemy, if they should appear, and acquire some sense of the size of the force. One of the pair is to run back immediately on contact; the other is to estimate the force, then retreat with the intelligence.

***

That done, I relax a bit. All the projects are proceeding well, and I deserve to spend a little time with Midnight. She usually helps setting up at the community kitchen in the big lodge, but I don't see her. One of the men working on the next meal tells me she went to search for some herbs to season the food.

"Probably to the big meadow to the south," he says.

I thank him and set off with a bounce in my step. I think a meadow is a nice place for a short break, especially with Midnight in it. As I reach the edge of the open space, I reflexively sweep my bow off my shoulder with one hand and grab arrows with the other as I take in the scene before me: two strangers are locked in silent struggle with Midnight. Nosey hangs by his teeth from one man's crotch. He seems to have a firm grip on his opponent so I load an arrow from my quiver and draw. I look first at Midnight, but she too seems to have her stranger well in hand, so I shift my aim to the one Nosey is trying to bring down. My shot enters the man's ear. He's done.

I grab another arrow and draw it back, but Midnight's disarmed man is on the ground with a knife to his throat. He holds very still on his back. The whites of his eyes display his fear and both of his empty hands wave in the air. A war hatchet lies nearby. Nosey and I are both at Midnight's side in a heartbeat and I scoop up the weapon. The stranger shifts his gaze from Midnight to Nosey to me.

Midnight rolls her captive over on his belly and holds her hand out to me. I release the tension on my bow, plant the arrow, and hand her a piece of leather strap. She binds the man's hands together and drags him to his feet.

Nosey cleans blood off his fur as I scratch his head. "Nosey deserves some treats tonight."

Midnight smiles agreement, then the smile changes. "So does Hawk."

I grin, she nods, and we head back to the village with the captive.

Chapter 16: Midnight Slave

We walk in the gate and people gather around, eyes bright with interest. I push through with the captive and Hawk behind me, watching. We march straight to the big lodge. We drag the prisoner to one of the carved story poles, where I pull some longer straps from my bag and tie him to the pole.

"Start a fire."

The prisoner's face pales to a bloodless white.

"What are you doing in our territory?"

"Midnight! You know me. Let me go and I will tell you everything!"

I push right up to his face, pitching my voice to a menacing whisper. "Yes, you will, one way or another. Start talking, from the beginning. If I believe you, I don't have to hurt you. If I don't, you can join your friend with the spirits."

I don't think he could seem more wretched, but he manages it.

"First, how many more of you lurk around here?"

"A few other scout teams, but we are only trying to learn where everything is. He ordered us not to be seen, but you walked up on us."

The story starts with what we already know. "Shaman wants to move west. He told us you have a lot more food, easily gathered, and the Winters are milder."

"So, we are all to be your slaves?" He hesitates, so I slap his face.

"Shaman promises rich lands and many slaves to all who follow him. The greatest warriors will inherit the new villages to rule as chiefs. Shaman said that with life so good, the villages will be easy to take."

"What do you think about that now, Sparrow?" I glare and tap my knife hilt impatiently.

Sparrow hangs his head.

"Leave him tied to the pole for the night."

Hawk asks me, as we walk back to the village, "Is he a typical warrior from your old people?"

"Probably. They are hunters, good in the bush and strong against animals, but they have never seen war. Neither have I."

He wraps his arms around me and holds me close for a time. After I soak in some of his comfort, I expand on my thoughts. "None of us have. I hunted food for the People. I do not want to hunt men and women, but I don't think they give us a choice."

The next morning, we walk into the lodge, straight to the captive. I look him over.

"Sleep well?"

"What are you going to do to me?"

"That *is* the question, isn't it?" I punch him once in the gut, right at the diaphragm, and stand stone-faced as the hunter chokes and gasps for breath. Silent, I wait for the captive to recover, staring straight at him. Nosey shows all of his very pointy teeth and chitters excitedly, like he wants to take a few bites out of the man.

After a time, Sparrow's gasps calm and I break the silence. "With the Chief not here, Hawk has to decide what to do with you. Or we could leave you here, like this, and wait for the Chief to arrive…whenever that may be."

Sparrow's eyes hold real terror. Several new wounds mark his skin where some local youths have taken a whack at him during the night.

"I have a proposal. Your freedom is forfeit—that is not at issue. You have a choice to make now."

I stop a moment to let that settle in. "I don't think the River People have any slaves at this time, but it is a historical tradition for both of our peoples that enemies become slaves when they are captured in battle. I would give you that option because we were once part of the same community. If you try to flee, your *life* is forfeit, and our hunters will find you long before you reach the Grasslands. You have seen that these are not the weak people that the Shaman told you they are. Choose now."

Sparrow looks straight into my eyes, judging whether I speak truth, then his head drops.

"I submit. We would have captured or killed you if that furry demon of yours hadn't split our attention. Shaman has offered a reward for you, or a recognizable body part. I won't choose death for Shaman's pride or ambition. By the spirits of my ancestors who have heard my words, I will serve."

I look at Hawk. He shrugs.

"Good. I believe the People need some help building fortifications to prepare for the attack." I hesitate for a moment. "Before we take you in, though, tell us what you know of the Shaman's plans. Why were you two in that meadow?"

Sparrow sighs. He seems to gather his thoughts, or perhaps he is deciding how much to tell us.

"We were one of several teams scouting this area. When the village got word that you were seen with three strangers, the Shaman feared you had fallen in with people from here. The trail is clear enough, after all, and now you have been declared an outcast from our People. Someone always watches your family. Shaman thinks we… they…should move sooner than Spring, as he previously planned. He still hadn't decided when I left. It may depend on other scout reports."

"How many warriors would he send?"

"All of them—about a hundred. If he decides to send the fishers and builders and some of the other people, that number could double, or more. He may also call on alliances. Some of the other villages' young men and women may be willing to join as an adventure."

I step forward to untie the straps holding Sparrow to the pole, catching him as he staggers, and help him to a seat on a tree round. I call one of the men who is working on breakfast for the crews. He hurries over.

"Nighthawk, would you please see this man fed, cleaned up a bit, and ready for work?"

"Is he free or slave?"

"Slave. He will help with the fortifications, then whatever other tasks that need doing."

Nighthawk looks the prisoner over. "He smells rank. I will have him ready in a little while. Where do you want him then?"

"Take him to Coyote, on the trench. They are almost finished, then he can start helping on the wall." Glancing at Hawk, he signs AGREE.

Out of earshot from the lodge, I stop. "If more scouts lurk around, we have to find them."

He considers. "Yes, we do. Can we set up some ambushes on the trail? Maybe send some as far as the halfway point? They can check anyone going either way."

"Good thinking. It's the best way to stop scouts, and I wish I'd thought of it. I'll send the teams out right away." I kiss him hard, stroking his face before I turn to my task.

***

Hawk walks off and I smile, then go cold again as a thought nags at the back of my mind. Given a quiet moment to think—and the information about a reward for me, either alive or in parts—a thought surges to the front. *My family is in danger if word reaches the Grasslanders that I participate on the other side of this war.*

I work it over in my mind for a while, coming up with ideas and rejecting them as not practical. Finally, a useable plan forms. I try to break it down and it seems like something that will work. I have a gut feeling that time is not my friend. In Fall, the weather can turn at any whim of the sky spirits. As it is, we might have poor conditions on the return.

I scoot back to the lodge and ask if anyone has seen Seabird or Boomer.

One of the cooks looks up. "Yes, they were here a few minutes ago. Looking for Hawk, I think. He's at the wall."

I thank her and hurry off to the part of the barrier where people are working. The construction is actually coming along very well. The fallers and trimmers started first, right at the beginning, and that has paid off. They have been able to keep ahead of the crew raising and setting the poles. The workers cleared the plateau of trees early on but have managed to keep up with the setters using new Song winches to bring poles up from below.

I arrive as Hawk listens to Boomer's report.

"We saw no one, but we did see signs that some have passed."

Feeling time pressure, I interrupt. "Hawk, excuse me. I have a plan, and I need these two. It relates to Grasslanders on the trail."

Hawk looks startled, then sighs. "What's your idea?"

"My family is under suspicion, as you know. I want to take Seabird and Boomer and lead those who want to leave to safety here. The other part of my plan is that we will make sure the trail is clear as we pass through. Any scouts we come across will be dealt with."

His face falls; his eyes reflect the struggle in his heart. "I don't want to risk you—we need you here. Look at what you did with the Grassland scouts, and how you handled the captive. *I* need you here."

"I know, but I need to see my family safely out of that village!" I shudder, a spasm that starts at my head and travels all the way to my waist.

"Shaman may decide at any time they are a danger. We know he will kill. I should be able to bring them out and be back before Winter if we leave now. We will also gain information from inside the village about what they are doing, and how soon they will be ready to move."

Hawk hangs his head. "What are you thinking?"

Boomer speaks up. "I understand Midnight's point. She probably has it right, and we don't need any distractions when this blows up. We have to see them safe because hostages make us more vulnerable. We don't want to contend with that when war comes. Let's bring them out of there, safe to our territory."

Slowly, Hawk nods and takes me in his arms, chin nestled over my shoulder.

"You must come back." His emotion burns and I share the heat of it. "I don't like this at all."

"Hawk, I will have your best men with me and we will be in and out before anyone knows. Two weeks' run, and two back. We should make it, hopefully before snow flies. I have to do this. If Shaman harms my family, I will always carry the pain, and the guilt…"

He hugs me again, then pushes me gently away. "Go on then and come back as fast as you can. Pack tonight and leave in the morning. I won't be happy until you are home."

He stops, thoughtful. "It increases the danger, but if your family knows of others who want to leave, bring them. Be very careful and make sure no one sees them leave. The best part of that is that you will have more people with you on the way home who can fight."

Seabird grins. "We will make sure everyone is like wood spirits, here one minute, then gone…including anyone who stands in our way."

Chapter 17: Hawk
Parting

I reach home shortly after sundown. Midnight spins around from whatever she is doing and rushes into my arms for a long passionate kiss.

Sometime later, we go over her plans again.

"I won't enter the village until night, when movement quiets down. My parents will know who are friends who might want to leave, but I have no idea how many will come. I may have to speak to people in their homes after dark. My father, mother, and sister should be able to talk to those we can be sure of. We'll stay a day and a night, and leave after dark as soon as we can move. I will take no chances that aren't necessary."

I grasp her hand and squeeze it tight. "I want to be with you when you are in danger."

She snuggles into me. "You can't be, this time. Boomer and Seabird will see me home to you again. So quit worrying and kiss me some more…"

Chapter 18: Midnight
The Rescue Begins

The sky starts to glow with the rising sun as I rise and give Hawk a nudge. Shouldering my pack, we walk together to the big lodge to meet Boomer and Seabird, who wait for us after finishing off a good breakfast of salmon, bannock, and berries. Hawk and I eat one bannock each, and I gratefully stuff a stack into my pack, along with some more smoked salmon and dried berries. We have already said our goodbyes in the night, so I kiss Hawk once more and start off, Boomer and Seabird on either side and Nosey in his pouch atop my pack.

***

We push ourselves, moving fast, and travel late into the night. I smile as we pass Hawk's Camp. We cover a lot of ground, camping light and rising early, and maintain a distance-eating pace, sparing no time for anything except to reach our destination. The days run together like one long dream.

Two seven-days pass and we close in on our objective. Abruptly one day, about noon, I call a halt, shed my pack, and release Nosey so he can stretch his legs. I motion for the men to join me on a flat piece of dusty ground and start drawing a map with a handy stick. As it takes shape, they see the River and the village—which is our goal. I keep drawing, filling out the details of the land around the village on the other sides. I mark rows of hills and creek beds, and finally throw my hands up to indicate that I'm done, holding the stick in my palm with my thumb.

The men examine the map and I point to a circle and softly whisper, "Shaman." I draw their attention to another circle near the northern edge of the village. "My house." They nod. I show them a spot to the southwest of the village. "Us." They nod again. I use the stick to make a series of dots from our position around the village, at a distance, to a place directly north of my family's house. Then I scuff the map away with the stick.

"Tonight," I whisper.

I lead them to the southeast across the River over a series of gravel bars, almost dry at end of season, then to a clump of trees at the base of a bluff that rises directly behind us. We drop our packs and Seabird digs out bannock and smoked salmon and passes it around. Nosey makes the rounds. I think perhaps he eats more than we do. He finally snuggles up to my pack and has a snooze.

Seabird signs, YOU TWO SLEEP. I'LL TAKE FIRST WATCH, BOOMER WILL TAKE SECOND WATCH. THEN WE'LL GO IN.

I raise my hand in agreement, then curl up next to Nosey and my pack.

In the late afternoon, someone slides a blanket over me as the Fall chill sets in. I wake enough to feel Nosey roll over and snuggle under the blanket next to me.

***

I awake in full darkness with clouds rolling in, devouring the moon and stars, and Boomer rouses Seabird.

I stretch, yawn, then prod Nosey and push him out from under the blanket so I can roll it up. We ready our packs for a fast pick up and travel, piling them under a big tree at the edge of the grove nearest the village. Boomer and Seabird follow me as I enter the outskirts and turn left, leading the way to my family's pit house. We go up the roof one at a time and climb down the pole, me in the lead.

I see my mother first and a quiet moan of relief comes from my gut. She spins about and hisses! Her shock turns to joy, but I note shadows of fear linger. She runs to me, wraps her arms around me, and sways back and forth. My father and sister pile in, and no one notices Nosey, Boomer, and Seabird climb down the pole. The men stand to one side, both grinning as they observe the reunion.

My father sees them first. "Who are these fine young men you bring? Is one your partner? Both?"

Boomer and Seabird look at each other and erupt in hushed chuckles.

I stand pole stiff for a moment, eyes wide, then surrender to a grin. "I have one man and he is enough for me. I had to leave him behind to make sure we have a home to return to." My smile vanishes. "I want you to meet him, but you all need to come with us. You won't be safe here for long when the fighting starts."

Smiles vanish and my mother says, "Let's talk."

I stop her. "Why did you look so frightened when I came down the pole?"

"Shaman and his followers stalk us anytime we go outside. It's petty intimidation, punishing me and anyone else who suggests the raids are wrong.

They have a hold on most of the community. If we don't support their plans, they harass us… Until now that's all it is, but it wears on us and we don't know how far they will go!"

Her voice rises to almost panic and I grab her in a tight hug. "That's why we're here."

We talk for a long time.

"I worried about you and the others every day since I left. Someone who can contemplate murder and slavery will think nothing of tormenting those who disagree with them. After that, it is an easy step forward to torture and murder. It is a certainty that they plan to use you and any other dissenters as hostages to weaken our resolve and force compliance. The Shaman has no boundaries to his hunger for power.

"I have found a new home for all of us, and any others who feel the same as you. Please say you will come with me."

Tears trail down my face and I reach one hand to my sister, Windflower, who reaches back, snuggling close.

Woodshaper, my father, slams his fist on the table. "Coolwater, Windflower, what do you say? I agree to Midnight's plan. The hunters will have their blood, one way or another. I don't intend to satisfy their lust with mine, or any of yours. You say the new village is strong and wise? Do they have food enough for all of us?"

Seabird steps forward to address him. "More than you have here. Our resources are plentiful, so long as you are willing to work for them."

"Then I favor the move. Coolwater?"

Mother looks deep into my eyes for a moment. "Very well. I've had a bellyful of what's been going on here. Let's leave before the war starts, and we can't. Windflower, you are the least conspicuous messenger, so you should go to the other families. We will make a list of who you should visit. Do not approach anyone not on the list, especially that boy you've been tormenting lately! His father supports the Shaman. If you two are meant for each other, then he will be here when all is over and decided.

"The new Chief, Hardspear, thinks a lot of himself. He supports the war and commands their warriors. He was chosen by the Shaman."

I nod, thinking about the time Hardspear tried to force himself on me. Nosey took a bite of his ankle as I whacked him with my staff. Last I saw, he still walks with a slight limp.

We agree on a meeting place—the grove where Seabird, Boomer, and I stayed this afternoon. My parents will meet us there before dawn, following the same route out that we used going in. They understand that action must be taken swiftly, or we risk discovery and disaster for all. The other families will make their own way as they can, following the blazed trail.

With time taken for hugs and thanks, we retrace our route out of the village, and soon we have left the most dangerous area. Amazingly, I saw no sentries anywhere! *That's not how I would handle security with a war looming.*

Chapter 19: Midnight Family

My loved ones and the others arrive in the early morning dark, ready to travel, and we leave immediately. We push my family to put some distance from the village before light. Moving as fast as we can, we slip into the rocky creek bed and follow it downstream. I've become used to bushes and trees being right close to the water's edge in River territory at this time of year. This feels very exposed, with just flattened dry grasses and the odd bush on the banks.

It's almost dawn by the time we finally achieve a comfortable distance from the village and move toward the trailhead. Boomer suggests we turn farther south and then cut back, in case our previous tracks were seen. We will use a different place to ford the River, a bit south of where we crossed before, and travel cross-country to the main track south. The other families following will meet us the next night.

We move fast and make a hide within sight of the route on a slight wooded rise. We will be able to look down on anyone traveling past without being seen. We shed our packs, ready our weapons, and wait, nibbling on cold bannock and berries when we feel hungry. Nosey wanders off. He returns an hour later, curls up on my pack and spends a while grooming himself. Satisfied with his coat's condition, he settles in for a nap. We all take turns sleeping, since we don't know when the other refugees will arrive.

The day passes and the weak Fall sun slides behind the ridge of pine-dotted mountains above us. The air is chill and thick with gray clouds moving in fast from the southwest. This night will be dark.

Seabird comes over to where I talk quietly with my family, catching them up on everything that has happened since I left. He tells me he's going down closer so we don't miss the families in the dark.

It is many hours later when I hear: "Hawk," the password the other families were to use. Seabird hoots like an owl and my mother and I walk down to the trail where Boomer has a group of about forty men, women, Elders, and children.

This was the most dangerous part of the rescue. If the refugees had been caught and forced to talk, a war party would be meeting us. We have managed to do everything we set out to do with no mishaps…so far.

My mother greets the people and leads them off the trail a little way. "Did you have any trouble getting away? No? Good. We have to collect the rest of my family and the men with my daughter. Wait, quiet. We will go soon."

I hear murmurs of agreement and sprint up the hill.

"They're here."

Everyone grabs their gear. I shoulder my pack and kneel to let Nosey climb up into his traveling bag. At the trail we exchange quick greetings and I stride off purposefully, leading the way southwest. I want our troop to be as far away as we can as quickly as we can, but it's slow going. Boomer takes point, feeling with his hands for the cut blazes on trees and feeling for the trail with his feet. Clouds have packed in and it's pitch-black now, so Boomer stops and waits for me to catch up.

"We need torches. Young and old are stumbling into, or over, things and someone is going to be hurt and slow us even more."

Seabird pulls one out of his pack. "I thought we might need them, so I made these today. Having all the pine trees around here made it quick work."

He digs a fire drill out of his pack and in a short time, a flame brightens the tinder and sparks the torch, lighting everyone's faces. Seabird pulls out another and ignites it from the first, then stomps out his little fire, digging deep to kill all of the embers. He kicks dirt and pine needles over the spot to erase any signs.

"You go first. I'll bring up the rear."

Boomer nods and sprints down the trail. The blazes glow on the marked trees and the path is clear to everyone now. The refugees look relieved and we are able to move at a fairly good speed now. I send the Elders to the front, behind Boomer, so they can set the pace, then I step aside and drop back to Seabird, who brings up the rear. I note he has cut a spreading pine branch and tied it to a leather thong fixed to his waist. The dragging branch wipes out our tracks. I smile at him and clap him on the shoulder. I unsling my bow and adjust my quiver of arrows to give me ready access. Seabird grunts approval.

***

An Elder at the front screams and people dive for cover. Arrows fly and I push forward toward the wounded woman, with more screams and the *thuds* of bowstrings pushing me faster. I see something at the side of the trail, pivot my aim, and catch a glimpse of Boomer's unmistakable physique. I turn to the other side, where a warrior is trying to drag one of the children off into the darkness. I let fly and nock another arrow, having the satisfaction of seeing the child run to her mother. I step off the trail where I shot at the warrior. His body is draped over a bush, motionless. After a moment of complete silence, people start to gather back on the trail.

I see Boomer at the front of the pack and join him. "I got one."

He replies, "I got one."

Seabird nods. "I did too. They seem to like three in an ambush now. Sadly, they learn."

I sense something more, another threat, and throw my hand up to catch their attention. I strain, but hear nothing. I recall a rockslide that comes right down to the trail not far ahead, which will provide cover for us if more warriors are in the area who might have heard the scream. Waving everyone on a bit farther, I call a halt and we seek cover behind the rockslide.

I quickly review the people and pick out anyone who might be helpful in a fight, making sure they are all armed. Seabird, the children, and the Elders move beyond the armed group.

We barely manage to settle behind the slide when a faint voice comes from back the way we came. *Someone must have spotted them leaving the village.*

"Hey, how long are we going to chase this bunch? If they don't want a share of the new lands, it leaves more for us! This stinking trail! We just finished running it and now we're back on it, going the other way. Let them go, I say. I need some happy time with my Cuddlebear." A short burst of barely muted laughter accompanies the whining.

Another voice rises: female. I think it's that mean woman I never liked, Redcougar. She always tried to bully us in the women's house, but together we shut her down every time. Some people are just malicious in nature.

"Shut up and run," she says. "We'll catch them up soon and I want first choice of the new lands Shaman promised. If you're in such a bad way, go on home, you whining shit."

I can't help but smile as I figure they're about close enough. My arrow is nocked and I pull the string back as I rise enough to aim. Her face turns back from berating her latest victim and she recognizes me, freezing for the second it takes for the arrow to travel and bury itself in her throat. *I'll feel no regret for that one.*

A quick count shows about twelve of Shaman's raiders remain, and shoot and move is their only option on the trail as we fire from the protection of the rockslide. Their numbers dwindle quickly, but two made a run for it after my first shot and I let them go. Perhaps their story will slow any further pursuit. Certainly Shaman will be more cautious in the future.

We turn away and run to catch up with the Elders and children. I prod the whole group on for a time to put some distance between us and the corpses—which are likely to draw scavengers—then stop to assess the wounded Elder. It's not serious and I pack the gash with healing moss, then tie a strip of cloth over it. She thanks me and says she feels able to keep going.

I realize now it will take a few days longer than I thought to reach Highwater. The Elders and young children can't keep up the same speed as we managed initially, and now we must move more cautiously.

When we are a good distance from the attack location, I give the order to rest for a while and suggest they try to sleep. Daylight will give us a better chance of spotting another ambush.

During brief stops, we have gathered dried grasses and strips of bark for a few torches. They will give us away in the dark, but we may have to march at night again at some point. *Best to be prepared.* We relax as best we can through the remainder of the night, starting out as the sky begins to lighten.

We travel most of the day, with rests as needed. When the sun falls behind the mountains, I call a halt and ask one of the young men, Brownrabbit, to find a place to camp out of sight from the trail where we can build a fire. He returns in a little while and leads everyone to a large flat space that is hidden by a scree slide from the trail.

We all drop our packs gratefully.

***

The new day dawns cloudy but dry as we gather up our gear and prepare to travel. I lead the way back to the trail and we carry on with the weather threatening, but it doesn't drench us. We carry on for five more days, cold and damp, and then the sun breaks through the clouds. We all feel a little better having a bit of warmth from the sky.

I scan the sides of the trail as I lead the way. Boomer brings up the rear, and Seabird scouts ahead. A whispering breeze follows an arrow going by, a finger's width from my nose. A *thunk* as it buries itself in a tree trunk is the only moment I have to move somewhere else. I drop and roll, pull and nock an arrow, rise to a squat, and draw and pivot to face the direction the arrow came from.

A flicker suggests my best guess as to where the shooter is. I aim my arrow at that area and it *whangs* off a tree. I have another nocked and scan for movement. I slide to my right and crouch as an arrow passes through the space I just left. I catch a glimpse of the attacker as they fire and wing my arrow to skim the tree they're hiding behind.

Arrow nocked and drawn, I slide left again, hoping to acquire a clear target. The attacker anticipates my move and swings around her tree, but she takes too long to find me. My arrow sinks into her chest and her arrow flies into the sky as she drops. The refugees lie flat on the ground. No one moves.

I hear another *twunk* of a bowstring, then a cry in the trees beyond the point where the first ambusher shot from. For a moment, silence drags. Seabird appears from the direction of the attack, waving his bow and two others above his head.

"Got two. I didn't see any more. They had a small camp back a way in the brush." He disappears the way he came—likely to gather the enemy weapons and supplies. Boomer comes in from the other side of the trail, catches my eye, smiles ruefully and shrugs. "Wrong side of the trail. At least we know it's clear."

Nosey chitters and draws my attention to my troop of refugees. I turn with my bow held overhead to reassure them. "It's all over. Let's go."

The refugees spring up and start running down the trail. "Easy!" I call urgently to them. "There were only three, and we got them. You don't want to rush into another ambush!"

My words sink in and they stop, all of them looking lost and confused. None of us have experience with warfare, but the hunters and I have had more time to wrap our heads around it. Most of the adults hunt and fight off predators, but this feels different, and it is. Warfare is more like hunting a killer cougar. You don't even know danger lurks until someone dies, unless you are very good and very lucky. I walk over to the crowd and put my hand on the head of a young girl whose wide brown eyes show white all the way around.

"This comes because of the evil you left behind. Your parents chose wisely."

Seabird appears, carrying three more bows and quivers of arrows. Refugees step forward to take the weapons from him, and he gladly passes them over. Several bags of food are entrusted to some of the unarmed people to carry, and three warm-looking blankets are distributed to the Elders. If they don't need them, they will give them to those who do.

Boomer calls from the rear of the troop, "All clear here! Now let's just trot for a while. We'll get there sooner in the long run." He smiles gently and we set out again, down the trail to home.

Chapter 20: Midnight Homecoming

We are all tired. The attack renewed our vigor, at least for a few days. The refugees are now sure they made the right choice, but it has been a hard march. The Elders are not used to this level of exertion, and the young have lots of energy for a while, but then tire from the sustained travel. We've had no more enemy incidents. It's only us and the trail, which has begun to seem endless.

The three white stones beside the trail that mark Hawk's Camp come into view, and I smile at the memories as a flood of relief flows through me. *We're almost home.* I very much want to see what he has accomplished at Highwater. I haven't let myself think too hard about him. I miss him terribly, but have had to keep focused on my other family and the refugees, and getting us all home safely.

I debate whether to push on and arrive after dark, or camp once more and rest for the night. I decide to ask the refugees, so I call a halt. They promptly collapse. Nosey climbs out of his bag and drops to the ground, staggering as he finds his legs. After a few minutes, Seabird and Boomer come in from their scout routes and I beckon them over. Half the troop is asleep with their packs still on by the time they reach me.

I gesture toward the three stones. "We are most of a day out yet." As I look around at the refugees, I see more are asleep now. "Do we push on or camp here?"

Boomer and Seabird both say, "Camp." I nod, and we set about rousing everyone and moving them off the trail. I show them the hide, suggesting that the youngest children sleep inside. They will all fit. Some of the people volunteer to gather wood. Our food is almost gone, but we have enough for everyone to have a small meal, and the scouts bagged a few rabbits and birds during the day. One of the mothers starts a fire with twigs and bark chips, while others spread out to forage for edibles. Seabird and Boomer leave to hunt, along with the men with new bows and a few more who brought theirs.

A couple of women scrape the duff down to the mineral soil and build three more firepits. I don't object. We are close enough to safety that I don't fear any more enemy scouts lurking around and if they are, several good people with weapons are roaming these woods right now searching for prey. Others are probably looking for us as well, if I know Hawk.

The hunters bring back a good meal for all, plus the excellent fortune of three Highwater scouts!

Seabird explains. "Kestrel, Lynx, and Longarm have been watching for us. Hawk sent scouts two suns ago, in addition to the ones looking out for Grasslanders. It's a wonder we didn't run across some before."

We feed the refugees and settle for the night.

I sleep all night with Nosey curled up next to me. Seabird and Boomer were stubborn about me sleeping. I have stood watches the whole trip, and they insisted they were not going to deliver a worn-out and exhausted Midnight to Hawk. Both grinned when they said it, so I gave in.

I awake from wonderful dreams of peace and throw back the blanket, prompting an annoyed screech from Nosey. I have energy again—*almost home!* I pack quickly, then look around to see who needs help. Others begin to stir and soon, the whole camp is up. I insist they wipe out any traces we have left, which is tough given the number of people who camped here, but we do our best. Then we trickle out onto the trail again.

Once the group is gathered, Seabird takes off down the trail and Boomer fades into the brush. Kestrel and Longarm likewise vanish into the woods on the other side of the trail.

Even the young children seem energized. A new village is ahead. Who knows what wonders they might see, and friends they might find? They march off excitedly as only the young can. Even the older folk show a spark of enthusiasm, colored by a little fear of the unknown, perhaps.

***

It is evening when we come within view of Highwater, and it is impressive. The top of the hill is surrounded by a high log wall, with the ditch and berm in front of it. Two tall doors stand open where a light bridge crosses the berm and ditch. Atop the wall, men and women with bows peer down on us. A torch as tall as a man burns on either side of the bridge on our side. None of us has ever seen such a thing. I knew the basic plan, but it's different when faced with the reality.

Someone on the wall recognizes us—me, at least, because I hear my name called out by a watcher. We pass over the bridge and enter the strange structure. It makes me think of an enormous lodge with no roof. Inside it still looks odd to me, and certainly does to the refugees, who have always lived in pit-house villages.

Inside we see a tall cedar-planked lodge with story poles at the corners, spaced along the walls, and beside the doors. A couple of the poles are carved and painted; the rest are in various stages of completion. Finishing the story poles after they're upright is not the usual way carvers work. Most are plain poles, left for stories to come. Houses, some finished and more in progress, fill much of the space inside the new village. We gape in awe. Even for Seabird, Boomer, and me, it hadn't looked anything like this when we left.

Word has clearly passed around the village of our arrival. As people flood out of all the lodges, I search the growing crowd of River People gathering to see us. Then I gasp and run, arms reaching and open for Hawk, also running to meet me. Nosey climbs out of his bag and leaps to the ground, so I dump my pack to wrap my arms around Hawk.

We come together in a great hug that lasts a long time while our spirits swirl together through our bodies. In time, we lean back and kiss. A great cheer rises, both from the River folk and the Grassland travelers. I take Hawk by the arm and pull him toward the crowd of newcomers.

"This is the next important part. You are about to meet my parents!"

Hawk's eyes dwell soft and warm on me. "It's an honor to meet them. They raised you to be who you are. That's all I need to know to welcome them."

I look up at him, tenderness and a little sparkle in his eyes suggests passion and mischievous plans for the night ahead back to me. I lead him by one hand to the refugees huddled in a group, looking lost and unsure what to do. Hawk raises his hands in the air and the People grow quiet. He speaks the trade tongue.

"My name is Hawk, partner to Midnight. Welcome, family and friends, to Highwater. We make a place for you here because of your courage and sacrifice, leaving your homes and all the history of your people on the land you hold dear, for the honor you hold dearer. You are not only welcome here; you are now part of our community. Family. As soon as it can be managed, we will celebrate the fact. For now, rest! Explore! Then we will show you to your new homes. You are welcome among us *as River People!"*

The River People roar their agreement and the newcomers bow their heads in recognition of the honor given. The used-to-be Grassland children scatter to explore this strange new place, which is *theirs!* Several stop to pet Nosey. When he rolls onto his back so they can scratch his tummy, I leave him to enjoy the attention and step forward, dragging my beloved by his arm, and speak to the adults in my party.

"Hawk is my mate. He found me, protected me, and treats me honorably. He is Chief of Highwater. Fisheagle is Chief of the River People, whose territory we all live in."

I pull him toward my parents and my sister, bouncing a bit with long-delayed excitement and relief at having them home. "My father, Woodshaper. Father, meet Hawk."

Hawk reaches out and grips my father's outstretched arm. "Woodshaper? We will talk later on that subject." He grins. "After you are settled and rested."

My father grunts. "Unless it is a crisis, that may be a day or so. That was a long hard run and some of us aren't as young as we used to be. I could sleep for a day or two, for starters."

Hawk laughs. "Rest! I see no arrows in the sky."

Smiling so hard my face hurts, I take hold of Hawk's arm again and drag him around. "Coolwater is my mother. She pushed me to follow my heart."

Hawk takes her hand with both of his and gives it a gentle squeeze. "I saw you once before, from a distance. You stood by your daughter as she shamed the Shaman with dirt and stones." He pulls her into an embrace and whispers, "Welcome and respect."

"And this is my sister Windflower."

Hawk touches his heart and smiles as he delivers a Song-style bow. "Will you grow as tall as your sister, do you think?"

"Perhaps, perhaps not. So long as I become as beautiful and smart as she is, I really don't care."

Hawk, and many others around us, burst into heartfelt laughter. I snort and hug her again. I've missed her, even her attitude.

Hawk steps back to address all the newcomers. "We must first get you inside and rested. We have an empty lodge that will hold all of you for now. It will have to do for a start while we sort out who will live where. We are still building." He turns to me. "I made sure the new house next to ours is ready. Why don't you take our family to it so they can settle in and rest?"

I smile and tug on my sister's hand. "Follow me to your new home. I know it seems strange at first, but you will soon be used to it. No more passing through smoke and climbing in and out on ladder poles. Here, you simply walk in!"

Chapter 21: Hawk Changes

While Midnight went to collect her family I've kept myself more than busy, which meant driving everyone else to be more than busy as well. Now she's back and I look forward to showing her all that we've accomplished. After sufficient time has passed for her family to settle in, I search and find her staring at the gate.

"Can I show you around?"

She spins around at the sound of my first word and hugs me again, then pushes me back. "I would love it!"

I signal the wall watch we are coming up and receive a wave in return. We stroll along the wall walk, the perfect place to observe all the changes.

"So, the ditch and berm are complete because I've pushed the wall teams to the point of exhaustion and dug a fair bit with my own hands. Good food, adequate sleep periods, and a healthy fear of not being ready when an attack comes kept my crews hard at it. When the last log went up into the wall, I ordered a day of rest and feasting. It so happened that was when the last of the People, and Fisheagle, appeared at the gate from Fishcamp. They entered with looks of astonishment. It is one thing to plan a completely foreign project—quite another to see it."

She chuckles. "Truth! I can't believe you got all this done while we were gone. You have many talents, besides being handsome and snuggly."

When I stop laughing, I pick up my story. "I showed Fisheagle all the new construction, answering questions and detailing what yet needed to be done. He was especially interested in the winches used to pull the logs up the hill, and the cranes made of logs and rope that also use a winch to raise and lower the wall logs.

"With the last arrivals from Fishcamp, around five hundred of the People are resident at Highwater, plus two Song advisors. The workers who were freed up from completion of the wall were directed to building a new lodge and twenty more family houses. I didn't know how many new people would be coming back with you. It pleases me to see I calculated about right. The houses aren't all finished yet, but they will be before long, and the newcomers can see they will soon have their own spaces. They can even pitch in and help."

Chapter 22: Hawk
The Sack of Clearwater

The first sign of trouble staggered in at close to midnight, two seven-days after Midnight brought the refugees home. Of all the scheduled hunters watching on the walls, it happened that Nightbird—so named because he has an extraordinary ability to see very well in the dark—was above the closed gate.

I relieve the Watch Commander, who is called "Granma'am" because of her muscular build and long gray hair. Some have called her a force of nature, like the wind or the River.

I reach the base of the ladder and start to climb up for my shift on the wall when I hear Nightbird. "One man approaches the gate!"

A frantic-sounding voice cries out, "Let me in! It's war! More of our people will come!"

I leap from the ladder to the ground, shouting at the gate watch, "Someone at the gate. Let him in, but cautiously!"

The gatekeepers unbar the gate, open one side enough to let the man in, then slam it shut and bar it again. Two more hunters close in and stand behind the gate guards, bows ready. The newcomer is pale, panting, and looks about to collapse.

Granma'am and I approach as he manages to croak a few words out: "Attacked…village burned, many dead…survivors come here. We heard…" He sways, crumples in a coughing fit, gasps, and tries to say more, but chokes. His clothing, scorched by fire in places and seeping blood from his wounds, tell me as much as he could have in his state. He carries a strung bow—the quiver is empty.

Granma'am grabs one of the gate men. "Find Fisheagle and bring torches!" She shoves the man away and turns back to the injured messenger.

The other gateman calls out, "I know him—he's Weaver, from Clearwater. He married my cousin, Starflower."

"Weaver! What happened?"

He struggles to speak but fails as his eyes glaze and his body goes limp. I place my hand on his chest to check that his breath still rises and falls. Granma'am peels off Weaver's shirt and leggings to look at his injuries. Two arrows are broken off behind the heads, one in his shoulder in front and one in his left side. He likely broke the shafts off himself, as they would have tormented him, bouncing as he ran. A deep cut seeps through his right leather legging. It's not pulsing, so it hasn't cut any big blood vessels. Granma'am rolls up his tunic and stuffs it under Weaver's head.

Chapter 23: Midnight Wounds and Healers

I hear loud voices—grab my weapons and run for the gate. A body lies on the ground. I note that Hawk is on the wall and ask a guard, Smallfoot, what has happened. She keeps to a short version and I survey the situation.

"We need a way to sound an alarm. We also need some torches outside."

Granma'am looks up at me and nods. "Smallfoot! Set torches some distance in front of the gate. Grab anyone who's standing around, and someone *please* send for the healer, if no one has already!"

Smallfoot starts grabbing people who have gathered to see what the yelling was about and sends them for materials. A row of torches on either side of the gate outside and beyond the trench begin to light the darkness.

More people come from their houses and lodges to investigate the uproar. Lynx pushes through the group around the wounded man with Greatheart, the healer, right behind him. Greatheart drops a bag next to the wounded man and rolls him onto his left side. With a cloth and a flattened wooden stick from the bag, he starts to probe the area around the first arrowhead. A twist and levering motion slides the arrowhead out.

He watches the wound for a moment, rips two strips from the cloth and folds one in half. Digging in his bag again he pulls out a smaller bag and extracts a clump of dry healing moss, rips off a small tuft and stuffs it into the wound. He covers it with the folded cloth and uses the other strip to hold it in place. He does the same to the other arrow wound and examines Weaver's leg. Then he packs it with more of the moss and binds it up as well.

He looks up at me. "That should start the healing. He needs a quiet place to sleep for as long as possible. He'll be fine in time." Greatheart turns away to shout, "Torches! I need torches!"

I look around for someone to move Weaver. "Seabird! Put him in the house they finished today and find someone to sit with him. We'll use it for wounded. If we need more space, put them in any structure with the roof done."

The healer nods. "I'll check him again later—I expect more wounded."

Freebird arrives with a blanket and we roll Weaver onto it. Four people carry him off to the house.

Hawk calls down, "Someone else comes…more than one. Open the gate— they are refugees!"

Greatheart spots a woman in the crowd by the gate. "Starfall! Bring cloth for bandages, clean water, and more of the healing moss from my lodge. You wanted to learn to be a healer? Now is a good time to start!"

She turns and sprints away as Greatheart peers around and chooses a quieter space away from the gate.

"Sweetgrass, we will set up over here!" He points to the area at the side of the main path. "Sundog! Take some people and acquire tables from the lodges. Set them over here." He gestures to the same area.

The gatemen swing one gate door open as I shout, "Send more bowmen to the wall! The enemy may be right behind them!"

Chapter 24: Hawk Refuge

Looking down, I see people with empty hands run for weapons, and the others who have theirs climb to reinforce us. More people emerge from the darkness and approach the gate and I shout down, "Grab one who isn't hurt too badly and have him, or her, watch for strangers in the bunch coming in!"

A guard signs understanding and moves to the gate as more people start coming through. About twenty have passed in when one of the Clearwater women screams and points.

"He's one of them!"

Five bows on the ground bend and center their aim on the man, another three on the wall walk. The invader makes the mistake of raising his bow toward the woman. He drops like a stone when eight arrows slam into him.

The archers turn back to the outside in unison and draw fresh arrows, nocked and ready. One of the River women approaches the corpse, pulls the arrows out, then climbs a ladder and delivers them to the wall watch, wiping the blood off the heads and shafts on her skirt. We spot and kill four more of the enemy who try to sneak in.

By now a crowd of Clearwater refugees stands at the gate, looking for strangers. Several refugees collapse of exhaustion and terror as they enter the safety of Highwater. Along with the seriously wounded, they are taken to Greatheart. A steady stream of refugees continues to materialize out of the dark. Finally, the stream becomes a trickle, then the odd straggler, most badly wounded.

"Close one gate!" I shout. Two men jump to the left gate and push it closed, then drive an arm-thick stake behind it, deep into the ground. Each gate door is as wide as the height of a tall man. A smaller opening lets arrow fire focus on a wide area from our side while protecting the guards inside. I see that most of the worst wounded have been treated by Greatheart and moved to the lodge. The healer and his assistants work on the lesser injured now.

Chapter 25: Midnight Tactics

Looking out of the gate, I notice the latest refugee appear out of the darkness and an idea stirs.

"Lynx, Kestrel—I can see only a short way up the Clearwater trail. I want a contained fire *on* the trail, a little beyond where we can see."

They run off to gather wood from the storage area. Looking around, I spot a group of six hunters who seem to have nothing to do.

"You six! Come here. I want you to split into two teams—one on each side of the trail, past the fire. If a small group of the enemy comes, let them pass, then take them down. If it's a large force, let them pass and join together to harass them from the rear. If the gate is closed, go to the back door and come in." They bare their teeth in a feral reply and run off.

It works exactly as I saw it in my mind. The first team got the fire burning, and then joined the six I sent. They split into two teams of four to bracket the fire from an easy bowshot away and disappear into the brush and darkness.

About forty warriors come down the trail and pull up short of the fire, clearly visible in its light. Eight arrows sweep in from either side and drop an equal number of the enemy. The remaining enemy warriors are frozen in shock for a moment, allowing eight more arrows find their mark before they think to move.

A swarm of arrows arcs out from the wall as the watchers see what's happening. The raiders are caught between the darkness that spits death and the wall, which does the same. Chaos sets in, and a few moments later, nothing living moves among that group.

We all wait…still, silent. Before long another group of about the same size bursts from the darkness into the light of the fire and the gate torches. They stop when they see the bodies on the ground, too late. Most don't last any longer than the first group, but a couple of laggers may have escaped.

The chaos stops again—we wait, checking for wounds, anticipating, ready.

A scout, presumably alone, comes into view, looks at the bodies, spins about and runs. One bowman on the wall takes a long shot and the arrow buries itself in the meaty part of the scout's shoulder. He staggers, trips over his own feet, but keeps running and vanishes into the darkness.

Hawk calls down from the wall, "Keep a strong lookout. They'll probably want to check us out in daylight. Wait for a little while, then send out a team to gather anything of use. Collect all weapons—arrows especially. I want guards on the scavengers beside the men already out. When we have everything, leave the fallen and come back inside."

I select several armed people and the hunters go out. After finishing their task, they call the ambush squad in and follow them through the gate, which slams shut and is barred behind them.

Tension hangs thick around me, so I climb onto a wood block and hold my arms up to draw attention. I let out a piercing, undulating cry that carries all of my fear, anger, and victory. I don't know where it comes from—it bursts out on its own. People stop in their tracks, eyes on me.

"Tonight, everyone followed orders. We wiped out the threat. This is what we can do! We have taught them to fear us!"

A bearlike snarl answers. The People are angry.

"No matter what they try, we will stop them. They have slaves and plunder in their minds. We have love for those with us. They cannot win."

Someone in the crowd starts the undulating cry I used. It is a little ragged, not something they have done before, but it seems to fit, somehow. Soon the whole crowd joins in and the sound builds and rises from the village as a scream of defiance.

I catch a glimpse of Chief Fisheagle at the back of the crowd and suddenly worry I may have usurped his role. I hop down and run to him, and he waits for me.

"Chief Fisheagle, I didn't mean to—"

He puts a finger to my lips to silence my apology. "Midnight, you said exactly the right things and I don't think I could do that war cry of yours if I practiced, which I won't. My role is to be a guide to my People but *you* don't need any guidance. A very old truth comes to me: 'Don't fix what works.' Keep it in mind when you are a leader. Speaking of which, I think we need a Warleader. We haven't had one for generations. I will announce it in the lodge at our next gathering. For now, keep doing what you do. Your instincts are excellent. Trust them."

David Oliver-Godric

Chapter 26: Hawk
Things to Do

Before the village sleeps, we tend to the wounded and make sure the wall is well manned. We do need an alarm of some kind to alert all of the People to an attack or other dangers. We have drums, but they are low pitched and I don't think the tone will carry far in the forest. I want something that will pierce the forest and let the people out in the surrounding area know trouble is at hand.

An ancient proverb says that the face of death triggers people to think about life and love. I suspect a few new lives began the night after the battle.

As the sun rises it casts a glow, even in our windowless house. I wake and lie warm and comfortable in bed and I reflect on Midnight's performance at the gate. She took command, then planned and executed a brilliant ambush with many moving parts. Afterward, she brought the People together before they had a chance to think about the carnage.

She has risen to every challenge thrown at her since we met.

Meanwhile, I lie there next to a gorgeous, tall, powerful woman with an appropriately devious mind, who loves me…

***

A bit later, while walking and thinking, I see Zizhan with Wei, the other advisor who arrived with Fisheagle and the last party from Fishcamp. I turn command of the wall over to one of the older hunters and climb down a ladder to talk to them.

After greetings, punctuated by the slight bow that the Song seem to appreciate, I try to explain my problem. Zizhan catches on right away. He is picking up our trade language fairly quickly, now that he has a feel for it.

He touches my copper armband and says, "Big dish make copper. Like copper drum—beat with stick. Make big noise. All hear."

Wei is not so sure. He speaks to Zizhan for a minute in their language, then Zizhan says, "Wei think another way better. He say long tube, like, make bigger sound with less copper. Copper, by itself, not so loud to beat on. He is right."

Smiling at their comradeship, I bow again to the Song men. I caught the qualified "by itself" about the copper dish, wondering what that means, and file it away for another day. Then I hurry off to find Sunshine, the coppersmith. She is at her house, where she has set up her workshop, and I explain what I want and why.

She nods. "It makes sense. I make little copper whistles and bells for the children sometimes. I'll talk to the Song and see if I can glean more detail from them on the best way to make it. We will need more copper to make one that will carry far. I don't have so much on hand, and you want to alert the whole village. I'll find Zizhan and we'll work it out."

One more issue is in good hands with Sunshine working with the Song advisors. I realize then I have been trying to do everything on my own. Midnight is back and has proven her leadership and tactical abilities. Chuckling to myself, I think she might even be better than me at tactics, if last night's performance is an indication. I hadn't thought of the fire ambush setup. I'll take it as a lesson learned. *I will have to be sneakier!*

Laughing out loud, I suddenly feel better about everything.

Chapter 27: Midnight Honors

In the morning, Hawk and I walk to the big longhouse, where the kitchen is set up. As we walk in, someone starts my war cry. It has become the sound of triumph to them. Everyone stops what they are doing and joins in—the sound of victory surges in the lodge and begins outside as well. Defiance roars again from our village.

I stand stock still, surprised. I have never experienced this oneness with anyone, except perhaps with Hawk, but this is different. Hawk puts his arm around me and squeezes. Looking at him, I see pride in me burning from him. Tears roll from my eyes and down my face. The People are one, including us newcomers. Even the Song advisors join in.

When the cry trails off, Hawk and I collect our breakfasts and find a place to sit and eat. The Song built a low table for their own use, and one of the local woodworkers liked the design and built a few more, slightly taller. They have caught on, and now everyone wants one. Before Highwater was completed, Hawk insisted defenses come first, but with most of that done, the woodworkers are cranking them out. Soon, every family will have a table, and the longhouse has several large ones so people can eat and talk together.

The cooks have asked for some taller tables for food preparation and they are slowly receiving them. The new furniture is sturdy, and the woodwork involves some techniques that the People haven't used before. The Song are frustrated by the lack of certain tools they are used to having, but to my mind, they make do very well.

Hawk sits next to Zizhan. "How long before Zahn returns?"

Zizhan looks up at the rafters, calculating before he speaks. "Two moons to Shanghai. A part moon to get ready. One, maybe more moons back…if weather is not too bad. Bad news is Zahn will probably wait until late Spring to leave. Cruel storms are common during Spring. He will want a shipload of furs and copper to make the trip worthwhile."

Hawk nods. *Three to five moons, and the ship has been gone two moons and a half.* The rains are settling in. When they start late, it usually means snow comes early. He bows his head.

"We need to build a heavy bridge over the ditch. It will be full of water from the rain and snowmelt in the Spring."

Zizhan dips his head in agreement. "Easy make bridge swing up with winches and bags of rocks or sand. One can raise the bridge when an attack comes" —he moves his arm with the hand straight and flat up and down to illustrate— "and lower it to let people out after. My people do this for all towns in the north. Dangerous people who ride *maa* to battle live north and east of us." Zizhan nods solemnly. "We will need big ropes. Bark strips will work well, but we will need many, and they must be made tight. I have made such ropes when I was younger. Need five, six strong young people. We can do."

Hawk smiles. I can tell he's added it to his list of things to do today. I believe he is happiest when his list of things to do is unreasonable.

I cock my head at Zizhan. "What is a *maa*?"

"Big animal: four legs, strong body, smart. Ride *maa* into battle, run messages. *Maa* very useful."

I nod and ponder what he has said. I tuck it in my memory for the future, then share my other thoughts.

"Considering the attack on Clearwater Village, we need to send runners to all the nearby villages soon, before the snow flies. They should all be ready for an alliance after this attack. We can teach them how to fortify their locations, as we have, and make pacts to help each other. We can also trade what each of us needs—arrows, for one thing—so we are all ready for Spring."

Hawk considers. "Perhaps we should call all the villages here for a potlatch and talk alliances."

"I agree. And we should send a runner to Rivergrass with the story of Clearwater and what we are doing to prepare. I think we need some work parties to start gathering copper, both for our own use and for when the ship comes back to trade. Perhaps Rivergrass can melt the copper out of the rock? We will need everyone who knows how to trap to fan out and gather many good pelts for trade."

Zizhan nods. "Good plan. Chen, at Rivergrass, knows how to make oven to melt copper. Send copper rock in canoes downriver, except what we need here."

Hawk looks at me. "Would you organize the bark-gathering and rope-making with Zizhan? I will send runners to coordinate the copper miners with Wei. We also need woodworkers to build the bridge. We'll see who gets to that last one first." He grins.

I offer him a competitive smile back. "I will organize the ropes, since the women are the ones who strip bark and work with the fiber, but why don't you put Boomer on the gate? And Seabird can organize the mining. We have many willing hands here."

Hawk smiles. "You're right. We can't do everything ourselves, and I need to check with your father about making molds for arrow- and spearheads, and with Clayshaper about what we need to make them hard… As soon as I start the runners on their way."

"Then we both have a day's things to do, so finish eating and go to work! But you should first see Chief Fisheagle and tell him what we are doing."

Hawk nods his head. "Yes, I didn't think. I'll do that first. He might even have some ideas of his own about what we should be doing!" I don't miss his wry admission.

"I'll go with you in my role as potential Warleader who makes ropes…"

Chapter 28: Hawk
Chrysalis

Fisheagle listens to our report. He asks questions when he isn't clear about something and sits silent for a while, brow furrowed. Finally, he looks up at us.

"You two have done and planned well. I think you waste time, though, conferring and then reporting here. We need to be together for these planning sessions of yours." He smiles wryly to take any feeling of rebuke away from his words. "Since you both seem to think best in the lodge, I will come there for breakfast. I can then hear everyone's thoughts firsthand. I may even have a few contributions of my own. I will choose one of the new long tables to be mine for meals. Many threads need to be woven together, and relations strengthened and defined with other villages, the Song, and more. You and Midnight are very strong in spirit, skill, and ideas. But I have lived long and seen more things. While that doesn't always help in this situation—where unthinkable things are being thought and done, for both good and evil—trust me, I may have some insights that will help us survive this crisis. You have accomplished much in a short a time. I believe you both will lead us through this conflict."

He looks down and I sense he is deciding how much to say. I've learned the Chief thinks deeply—and doesn't always share everything.

"I see our world changing, for us and our children, perhaps all the People everywhere. The Song, and this war, will change us in ways I cannot foresee. I think about our culture as being a caterpillar preparing for its great change into a butterfly or a moth. It feeds long, and only when it is ready, it makes a chrysalis for its great change. We are at that point. It takes time for us to develop into the next version of ourselves.

"It is my task to see we are still strong in our traditions and beliefs when the evil is gone so we emerge as still the People, connected to this place, our ancestors, our traditions, and the spirits who have guided us through time beyond our knowledge. But our future must now be as butterflies soaring through the skies and among the flowers. Let's work together and see what the future holds for us. I have sent scouts to Clearwater Village to see what is left, and if the enemy remains in the area. We may have to send a war party, and either way, any wounded must be brought here for safety and treatment. You need to learn to think of all the 'what-if' possibilities in every situation. The skill comes from being able to sort them from 'near certainty,' which will have to be addressed immediately, to 'not likely, but possible.'"

I shake my head. "Chief Fisheagle, I will always treasure your wisdom and counsel. I apologize for not coming to you sooner. I've been afraid that I've been overthinking things. I see now that I must speculate and analyze even more deeply."

The Chief snorts. "You are at the peak of your strength, both of mind and body. Keep doing what you have been! Wisdom comes with age and experience, and too often mistakes and failure are our teachers. I merely ask you and your key people to have breakfast with me. Now you both have a lot to do. You had better begin. Speaking of consultation, I will send runners to Rivergrass and the other villages, perhaps even farther afield. It is time for alliances." His eyes sparkle. "And listen to that woman of yours! I still think she is smarter than both of us."

Midnight grins and I take the older man's hand in both of mine. "We'll be in the longhouse for breakfast tomorrow."

Chapter 29: Midnight Defeat by Tree Bark

We search for Boomer and Seabird and find them at the gate, talking intently together. Hawk explains the plan and their roles. Both agree, then Seabird makes a face.

"Those bodies are starting to bloat up. It'll be a real mess and stink before long, and we'll be overrun by scavengers. The crows and ravens are all over them, and we see larger carrion eaters moving in. They need to be buried…now, and we'll need warriors to keep the scavengers from attacking the workers."

Hawk nods. "We can also burn them. I'll find someone to organize a disposal party. You'll start to work on the gate with Wei?"

Both men agree. They march off to draft anyone who doesn't already look busy and I see them lead about twenty people with tools out of the gate toward the ripening corpses.

***

The process of stripping cedar bark for the ropes is new to me, but I learn the women usually do it in the Spring when the sap is running through the inner bark. They say it is still doable in the Fall without hurting the trees. It will take more work to separate the dry surface bark from the inner, which yields the strong, flexible fibers for ropes. I learn that Fall harvesting is easier on the trees, if harder on the workers, because the tree shuts down for Winter and will lose less sap, healing by Spring. The process takes time, and I want the fiber ready for the ropemakers as fast as possible.

I only last a day at the task. My strips tear off too short, while theirs are very long, breaking where the ladies want them to, high on the towering trees. We didn't have many cedars in the Grasslands, but we had lots of grass, so our string and rope was all made of leather or braided grasses. I can make a great grass rope for snares, or headbands and such, but the cedar bark defeats me.

These women have the skills we need, and I now realize it's a skill I don't have. That's my excuse. Defeated by a tree.

I'll check on them every day to see if they need anything…and to cheer them on. They're really good at this!

Chapter 30: Hawk
From Peace to Pain

I arrive at Midnight's parents' house and find her father outside, looking a bit lost. I fear he has felt like a surplus person the last few days.

"Woodshaper! I was looking for you. I need your help."

He looks relieved and interested. "What can I do?"

I explain my idea for molds for arrow and spear points. "We need very many of both if war comes, and it looks like it will. Now the enemy knows it won't be easy, and I think they must wait until Spring before trying us again. If it were me, I would be working on ideas about how to breach the walls and gain entry to attack us.

"Regardless, we need a lot of arrows and spears. The shafts are easier, and most of us are pretty good at it. It's the points that are a problem. It takes a skilled flaker a long time to make each stone point, and not a lot truly have the feel for it. I've been talking to Clayshaper about making pottery heads for both arrows and spears. She needs a carver to make wooden molds so we can make tens of heads at once. A carver can make those molds very quickly. We have a few carvers here, but I thought you might like to take the lead on that project."

Woodshaper's face lights up. "I would be proud and thankful to be working on it! Will I not take that away from one of your own People?" The worry is back on his face.

I place my hand gently on the older man's shoulder. "You are one of my own People. Did you not hear Chief Fisheagle say it? You will find that we mean what we say around here. Are you not also the father of my partner? You are home! Your whole family has been more than welcomed by the River People."

As I speak, I see the strength and pride flow back into the man: his back stiffens, head rises, jaw sets, eyes burn with life and purpose. "I'll grab my tools. This sounds like a very interesting project! I need to speak to Coolwater for a moment, then I'll meet you… Where?"

"The lodge, and I'll take you to Clayshaper." We clasp arms and I feel the strength in him. I turn and head for the longhouse. As I reach it, a hunter exits

Fisheagle's house and breaks into a long stride out the gate. Events that were merely ideas this morning are actions by midday!

Everywhere I look, purposeful activity creates our future as the People rise to the tasks they've been given. Their industry serves the community, and their families. I see no rivalries, no conflicts, no selfish maneuverings. The People work as one entity against a power that seeks to crush and enslave us.

I enjoy a surge of pride, rudely interrupted when an arrow *thuds* into the ground in front of me. I hear one scream of pain, then another.

Chapter 31: Hawk
The First Battle of Highwater

I peer at the sky and track an arrow in flight so I find some clue where they're coming from. *There's one, and another.* The watchers on the walk fire back as fast as they can in all directions. We're surrounded.

Sprinting to the nearest ladder, I scramble up. On the ground beyond the gate, I spot a mere twenty or so shooters, so I run the walk. By the time I return to where I started, my estimate is no more than 100 bowmen arc their arrows blindly into the village.

Our People on the ground are screaming for anyone without a weapon to take shelter, so I dismiss that worry and fidget unsuccessfully with a defensive plan until the gate creaks. I trot down the walk and see one door slightly open and hunters leaving in small groups of five or six. They run straight out to the treeline, where they disappear from my sight. Scanning around to see who's directing the action takes but a moment. It's Midnight, bellowing orders right and left. As the People hear what needs to be done, they leap to obey.

An arrow *thunks* next to my foot and I move, quickly. Turning to the nearest ladder, I slide to the ground and sprint to Midnight. I touch her arm and she spins to face me as the warrior: dark focused fury and cold calculation. A spark of brightness blossoms in her fierce eyes that has nothing to do with the excitement of battle.

I lean close to her ear. "It's a harassing attack. About a hundred stretched out all around the village."

She nods and her eyes become distant, thoughtful, then narrow into focus.

"Boomer! Teams of six. Have them split into two threes, spread to catch the shooters in crossfire. As many teams as you can muster, some close, some farther out. GO! Find me on the walk where I can see what's happening, if you need to."

Boomer organizes anyone with a bow and some arrows and sends them out in alternating directions: one left, one right. Some stay close to the wall; others go into the trees, then spread out in a circle. Everywhere I look, people run for weapons or arrive at the gate armed. They keep coming, a river of men and women with cold, purposeful eyes, and Boomer keeps sending them out. Each wave goes farther before they turn around the wall, alternating from the group ahead of them as they make the circle.

I observe the counterattack and shake my head in wonder. It is all so right and I hadn't thought of anything along those lines. *She must see it in her mind as the battle flows.* I watch Boomer exit the gate, massive warclub in hand. He must have seen or felt a need to be in the fight. Midnight has her feet spread as she commands it all, lips tight in a straight line, intensely focused but emotionless as she shouts orders and watches how they are executed. She's a rock, solid in the face of chaos.

***

Arrows stop falling inside the wall, but outside, the battles continue face-to-face. A Highwater woman trips a Grasslander with her bow, an empty quiver on her back. She drops the bow, pulls her belt knife, and grasps it with both hands—arms extended above her head. She stretches forward, falling. Her entire weight drives the weapon through tough bone and cartilage, deep into his heart. Dark blood erupts in fountains as she rolls away and leaps up, knife in hand, the enemy's gore dripping from her hands and tunic.

She screams as she runs toward two more attackers. One goes down with someone else's arrow in his eye and the other backs away from the bloodstained horror now focused on him. He trips over another corpse on the ground. She seizes the chance and that nightmare creature leaps at him.

A short distance away, two of the enemy bracket Boomer, who wields his heavy warclub with skill. He swings full force toward the one to his left, seeming to miss as the club passes in front of the man's chest, causing his opponent to step back. He keeps turning and the club shatters the neck and shoulder of the Grasslander's partner, who moved in to what must have looked like an easy kill. Boomer's feet stuck, he spins in reverse before the first foe can react, swinging upward in a reverse arc from below, into the man's jaw, snapping his neck back at an impossible angle.

Cries of pain and anger come from our warriors on the gate. A wave of Grasslanders charges the gate, firing arrows as they come.

"They aren't giving up easy!" Seabird shouts as he raises his bow and drops attackers through the open space. I whirl toward the new attack and Midnight shouts what sounds like a Song word at Wei. He raises his heavy bow and fires a strange-looking arrow straight up. Embers trail from it as it flies higher, then bursts into a multicolored flower of sparks, dying as they fall.

The outside teams appear behind the attackers, firing as fast as they can. Some are out of arrows and charge the enemy with hatchets and knives. A group of fresh archers from inside come running and pour arrow after arrow into the attackers. They drop their bows, arrows gone, and draw knives and hatchets and close with the enemy. Blood sprays as the attackers, and a few of the River hunters, go down. But more and more of the teams sent out earlier—their task of clearing the first attackers done—come running back in to take their own toll on the Grasslanders.

***

Finally, quiet rules the battlefield. The ground in front of the gate is a blanket of dead bodies, which I soon discover extends all around the Highwater wall. Living warriors walk among the fallen, prodding to check their status. Climbing the ladder to the wall walk, I tour around it. I see some friends, and a couple of cousins. The rest are Grasslanders. I quit trying to count the bodies; I'll leave it to the burial party.

Looking up, thankfully I see dark, gray clouds coming in to wash the blood into the ground, and the bodies of the warriors will be clean when we collect them. I fervently hope the Grasslanders have been convinced to go home. Winter comes—they have tried and failed two times. If it were me, I would have waited for Spring. But I have no desire to be a Warleader.

The big surprise is that Midnight, very definitely, is a Warleader. I remember our meeting: her throwing dirt and stones at the Shaman, falling into my arms as she was on her way to warn us of the coming war. *The right place at the right time.* On the walk, above the carnage, I kneel and thank my ancestors.

Chapter 32: Hawk
Aftermath

We are gathered in the lodge. Midnight runs to Boomer as he enters. "I saw you in the battle. You got between two of them…and took them both out! I will never forget that."

"Neither will I. Death walked here today, and I was one hand." He shakes his head. "My ancestors spoke to me. I heard their whispers in my mind as I fought, telling me what to do."

She wraps his huge body in his arms. "You helped save us. Speak to those who guided you. I too hear the wisdom of someone much older and wiser when I fight. They speak to us so we can save our People. Now sit and eat. Spend some time with those who were out there with you. They will have similar feelings, and hurt shared is a burden lightened."

We all work on the cleanup once we are sure any surviving invaders have fled. Of the wounded, our People have been taken to a large house that Greatheart set up as a treatment room of sorts. Wounded Grasslanders, the few who survived, get patched up last. A handful of those expire before the healer can see to them. The remaining twelve are tucked in a wicker pen that is currently not being used. Armed and angry men with cold eyes stand guard.

The Grasslanders lost seventy-three dead, plus the captives. Their corpses are put on a sledge, or Zizhan's new device, and dragged to a swampy depression away from the village to rot in Spring. The captives will cover it with soil over the next few days, as other tasks allow. The River dead number fourteen, with about forty, more or less, wounded. The families will wash and wrap our dead for burial tomorrow. Today, we honor them.

The attack was awkward, to put it mildly. The Grasslanders surrounded the village, stretching their raiders fairly thin, then they had to loft their arrows blindly over the ditch and the wall and hope they hit someone. When the River teams sallied out, using Midnight's tactical approach to counterattack, the Grasslanders were slaughtered in their attempt to reach the gate for a push into the village. Those who did make it to the gate were targeted by archers on the wall walk, as well as by the ground teams.

***

The four of us, myself, Midnight, Boomer, and Seabird, head to the longhouse. Fisheagle awaits us, but insists that we have some food and unwind before we talk. "I'll be back soon enough."

I feel something short and furry rub against my leg. Midnight reaches down and scruffs Nosey. He jumps up between us on the bench and, of course, we obligingly make room. Petting and scratching him is a comfort to me, a bit of normalcy and contact with another living thing after the dying and chaos.

One hand still busy with Nosey, I glance at Midnight with a little grin. "So, tell me about that signal arrow."

She smiles slyly back. "You were taking way too long to put your alarm in place, so Wei and I came up with our own. We tied a birch-bark tube filled with some of the fire powder to an arrow, took a thin strip of dry bark, rubbed it with fire powder, and pushed it into a small hole in the tube. I'd already given instructions to our outside warriors that if they saw it fly, they should come to the gate as fast as they could. Wei lit the bark strip with some coals we had burning in a clay dish and fired it up where everyone could see it. *Poof!* Alarm given." She flashes a big toothy grin.

I shake my head in admiration and squeeze her hand. "Brilliant. Does that mean I don't need have my giant copper whistle made?"

Midnight chuckles. "Thanks for that." Her grin fades and she becomes serious. "We have only what is in the one keg of fire powder, and we don't know exactly how much we will need for mining copper. We can't make more until the Song return with the special salt, so no point trying to gather sulfur and coal until Spring. But I have already told the scouts to watch for deposits of either. We asked other villages locate areas with them as well so we can gather it quickly when Spring comes. The new slaves can help with that."

She shifts uncomfortably, but her voice is steady and her expression firm.

I nod. "Our way of life changes."

Everyone around us signifies agreement. Some shake their heads in perplexity or disbelief that things have come to this. Already we see big changes, like the village wall, which has to be manned with lookouts at all times.

Mining will start soon. It has never been an important skill, except for a few artisans. Hunters become warriors, miners, and many other things, which means we need more hunters. New arts and skills acquired from the Song change how we do many tasks, some traditional ones. Perhaps eventually we will learn how to find and work the gray metal that they use so much of for tools and other things. Every day it seems new ideas and ways of doing things move us in subtle and unforeseen directions.

Chapter 33: Zizhan
The Wheel

I realized early in my time here that the natives don't know about what the Song call *gu*. They haven't really needed them before, as their sledge works better in rough and varied terrain, but in the flattened ground around Highwater, and for the port, *gu* will be an advantage.

I built a big wooden box and fastened two poles crosswise on its bottom, one across the front and another at the back. The *gu* attach to the poles. Midnight let me use her auger to drill the peg holes—the pegs hold the *gu* to the cross-shafts.

I made the tree rounds from a downed bigleaf maple, well cured: it is a very hard wood. When it was fully dried, I worked them to almost perfect roundness. Next I attached a long pole to the full length of the bottom of the box that ends flush with the back of the box and stretches out in front. I have attached a crosspiece for two pullers, as the natives have no domesticated animals. The cleanup crew used it first to collect the wounded and bring them to Greatheart, and then to haul some of the bodies away. It will not be as good as a sledge on rough trails, but on the flat ground in and around the village, it is a huge help for heavy or bulky loads.

Chen and Li have introduced *gu* to Rivergrass on the flat river delta. They will build a wharf for Zahn's ship, if they have any time to do so. The more time I spend here, the more opportunities I see to make the People's lives better. Not that they complain. Their culture has struck an interesting balance in this place that provides so much. They are a product of the land they live in. I begin to understand…

Chapter 34: Hawk
Valued Allies

The potters are learning how to fire the new clay weapon points more than once to make them harder and more durable, and Wei showed us how to use sandstone to carve and shape the first-fired clay before the final firing hardens it even more, so they are perfectly shaped and hard as river stone. Now he teaches us how to build special ovens that burn much hotter to create even stronger pots and arrowheads, and in which to melt copper, even prepare food.

Zizhan has mentioned they miss the tastes of their foods from home. He tries to describe the flavors, but quickly runs out of words the People can understand. I suddenly realize the Song must feel out of place. Waving the others in, I raise the issue.

"Wei and Zizhan have saved many lives with their new ideas." They murmur agreement. "So, we should do something to show how much we appreciate them. They have risked their lives with us, and I know it has been a hardship for them, not having the foods they like to eat and many other things we don't even know about."

They all agree, but we don't know what to do.

Boomer speaks up. "Take it to the Chief. If anyone here can figure something out, it will be Fisheagle."

That gains everyone's agreement. I look around the table and realize they are all focused on me again. "All right, I will." I stand, bend to nuzzle Midnight's head, revel in the smell of her, and go to find the Chief.

Midnight lays a hand on my arm to stop me. "Before you go, I have something else I want to bring up. Fisheagle won't leave."

She looks at Boomer, and then Seabird. "So, what happened to the scouts on the blaze trail who were supposed to warn us if Grasslanders came in force?" Her expression is joyless, harsh.

Seabird pushes himself up from the table. "I'll send some fresh scouts out to have a look both ways on the trail. Some can go straight to the nearby villages on the north side of the River: Xwelich, and up to Chawathil, perhaps Spópetes as well. We should check south to Sq'éwqel to make sure they didn't find the long lake or Hidden River. No reports have come of the enemy crossing to the south side. We should have done this after we learned about Clearwater."

He shakes his head. "I haven't heard of anyone missing, but the Grasslanders may have made new trails. I'll find out."

Midnight looks Seabird in the eyes. "Don't go yourself. You were in the thick of the fight and need some rest. Find some who weren't and send them off, then come back here for food, or go straight to your bed!"

Seabird nods thankfully and walks out.

***

I locate Fisheagle watching the last of the enemy dead being hauled away. As I explain my thinking about the changes for both the People and the Song advisors, the Chief's bushy eyebrows rise.

"I had not thought of either of those things yet. Too many threads in my hands, I suppose. You're absolutely right. We all need a potlatch—tradition will help our People. Those who have lost family and friends can grieve, and we will share everything with the Song as guests of honor. Without their knowledge and advice, we would have suffered greatly. It won't be the same for them as having food from home, but it is the best we can do.

"We should wait a few days to make sure we don't face another attack."

"Good thinking, much like a young leader…" Fisheagle's face splits in a huge grin, and I suddenly feel very uncomfortable. He has something on his mind that involves me, and he's not telling, yet.

"A runner reported that the bodies of the missing scouts were found on the trail—they can now be honored with the others. It will take time to prepare. I will see to that. We found a larger number of Grasslander bodies as well. It seems they do not honor their dead."

His expression is grim. "By the way, you haven't asked about what we found at Clearwater. We managed to locate about thirty people who escaped, but twenty are dead. The rest of them may have scattered. The raiders are gone—back to the Grasslands, I assume. What they couldn't carry, they spoiled. The houses are all burned, and the story poles pulled down. We still look for more survivors."

"Thank you." A thought occurs. "Suppose we invite delegations from all of the villages around, both up- and downriver all the way to Rivergrass. Perhaps a Council of Chiefs? They can celebrate with us and see the preparations we have made. After Clearwater, they must know that any of them could be attacked next. If they see the wall and some of the new ways of doing things for themselves, it may help them survive. If I were a Grassland leader, I would think about attacking more of the undefended villages, not the one with the big wall that has already cost so many lives."

Fisheagle nods thoughtfully. "That makes sense to me. I hope the Grasslander Shaman is sane enough to agree. If he hates for the sake of hating, or if greed owns his heart, reason may not guide his actions. But you're right. The potlatch will be a chance to form solid alliances and help more of our People in other villages survive until Spring. Perhaps we can share resources as well as knowledge. I'll think on these ideas. The People should see us working together on their behalf."

I reach out and grasp the Chief's forearms. Fisheagle returns the gesture with a smile that speaks to deeper thoughts as well.

***

Walking to the longhouse, I find everyone still talking, except Seabird, and slide onto the bench next to Midnight to share what the Chief said about Clearwater Village. Grim faces look back at me. Then I tell them about the potlatch to bring some cheer to our People and honor our new members and guests.

"It is the best we can do for them, and the Chief is right. We all need to celebrate our community and traditions and make the Song and the refugees who joined us feel a part of who we are. We will grieve for the dead and celebrate the living."

All at the table, plus more than a few nearby who have been listening, express approval.

I look around. "Seabird?"

Midnight answers, "He should be back soon."

"Part of my thinking is that we should finally be left alone long enough to start on some of the projects I have in my mind. It also occurs to me that all of our experts in the various skills and trades will be right here, so when we talk about a particular problem we are having, someone may have a solution, or even part of one. Instead of fragmenting our skills into separate groups, let's bring them together."

The loud murmur of agreement surprises me. I look around and see at least half the village has listened and seemingly like the idea.

We spend the rest of the day cleaning up, repairing, and gathering arrows and other weapons from inside and outside of the wall. Scouts find no fresh evidence of the enemy. Dark, heavy clouds scud in and a misty rain begins to fall. Sunset comes earlier every day, and everyone shows signs of exhaustion after the battle and cleanup. The weather echoes our mood.

The consensus in the longhouse at dinner is to have a good night's sleep and start again in the morning. Boomer sets the watch schedule for the night and designates watch commanders for each shift to raise an alarm if trouble appears. Then we head for bed.

Chapter 35: Hawk
The Way Forward

Dawn arrives, dark and damp, but brightened by the knowledge that Boomer has resolved our alarm problem. He decided to use the biggest ceremonial drum in the village as an alarm and signal drum to rouse the People. The Song fire arrow is useful in a battle, but we have little of the fire powder to spare. The drum is more than a tall man's height across and large enough for eight or ten drummers to sit around it. We have agreed to sound it with a fast beat for an attack and a slow beat for morning call. Many of the ceremonial drummers volunteered for the duty. I hear that the drummers make new songs to accompany the calls. The slow beat rings out with a new song, and the village begins to stir.

Cooks arrive at the longhouse, build up the fires, and start food preparation. The first day watch heads to the wall to relieve the last night watch, whose members trot to the longhouse for warmth and food. Chief Fisheagle strides in and sits at the biggest table, a long slab of maple in the center of the building. Midnight and Nosey arrive right after, followed by a steady stream of the People. Midnight's parents and Windflower sit to one side of her. Boomer and Seabird arrive next, with Zizhan and Wei behind, and the longhouse continues to fill up. Soon all the tables are full and latecomers take places on the floor, as they used to do.

Fisheagle stands when the stream of the People slows to a trickle, and looks around the longhouse, smiling. "I think we need a bigger longhouse, and more of these tables!" Laughter answers him back.

"I want to say to you all…" He hesitates as if to gather his thoughts. "You have made me proud. I will stand with my head high in the company of other chiefs because of what you accomplished. Yes, much remains to do. But I think of the men and women who stand watch on the wall at night so we can sleep peacefully. I contemplate the warriors who were hunters not long ago, and still must be both. And what of the newcomers from the Grasslands—Midnight's family and friends—who abandoned evil to join us? The Clearwater survivors who lost so much? The Song, who share their people's knowledge and our battles with us? We have become much more than what we were, which was pretty good as it was, I thought."

He chuckles and the assembled people roar with laughter. "We are richer as community for those who have joined us. Keep these thoughts in your minds as we do what must be done to survive and thrive. All of our ancestors, even those of our Song friends, watch what we do now with as much pride as I have."

He takes a seat and I stand. "I try very hard to keep track of all the things that need doing." I clear my throat, still raspy from sleep. "If I forget something, can I be sure you will remind me?"

That spurs another burst of laughter and vigorous nods of agreement. It is wonderful that these People, with all that has happened, can laugh so freely.

"One of the things I worried about was the number of arrows we needed to hold off the enemy. They solved that problem for us for the short term, at least. We recovered hundreds of new arrows from the battle, most of which were stuck in our walls, or the dirt."

My audience responds with many smiles and nodding heads, recognizing the irony of my point.

"But we have many other tasks that we must complete. Some are our usual chores for this time of year, while others are new. I thank you now for your efforts."

Having run out of things to say, I sit down, reflecting on how awkward my address felt, but the time for speeches is over. Breakfast is next. Then the doing of all that needs to be done.

***

The People take time to eat and trickle out to their tasks. The leaders and a few others stay.

Chief Fisheagle glances at me. "I heard you say you struggle to keep track of all our various projects. That's understandable as priorities keep changing, so this may be part of the problem. Another part is that we've experienced more life-altering changes in the last few months than the People have seen in generations. I touched on it in the words I spoke to them. We also have many new members of our community who are not yet sure how they fit in."

I nod. Midnight's father and some others haven't settled as well as I hoped. Fisheagle continues.

"We will have a gathering of all the newcomers tonight to start to know each of them, and to discuss what their roles should be. But even our traditional roles are evolving with the circumstances, and with our new knowledge comes yet more levels of complexity. So far I see the new ways and tools as progress in new directions. Nevertheless, we must find ways to set goals and keep track of how they impact our society.

"We must also be able to modify priorities as our needs change. Up to this moment, we have reacted to the enemy, not counting Midnight's forays. She has shown me that we must think ahead of him—make him react to us in ways we can foresee and plan for. I can do that on a smaller scale, but now we are talking about alliances with all the villages of the People, the Grasslands, and we have also spoken of an alliance with the Haida…perhaps others. We have never thought in this way before. We have traded, yes, but now we must build alliances between many peoples.

"My mind is muddled by trying to imagine how we might make that work while we remain true to ourselves. What if we cannot survive as our own distinct culture? Are new tools going to change us and our beliefs?"

Fisheagle has taken us on a mental journey that I never thought to contemplate, but events have opened new trails. He continues.

"We spoke to the Haida trader, Ts'aak, about an alliance, but they are a great nation along the coast on a group of islands, and on the mainland a long way north of here. Why would they ally with a single village so far away? But if we can organize all of the nearby villages—first for defense, but also for trade—then we may have something of interest to the Haida." He lets that work in our minds for a moment.

"We, the Haida, and the Nisga'a on the mainland also, have the new tools and different ways to build, mine, make pottery, and who knows what else we may learn from the Song when they return. Right now, we are sharing that information with those in need. Perhaps we should be careful with the new knowledge. If so, how? It is likely the Song merely trade along the coast. We know from our inland trade routes that some tribes—either from need or, like the Shaman—prefer to take instead of trade. Keep this in your minds, all of you, as we plan our path forward."

Midnight chuckles respectfully. "Chief Fisheagle, you see a bigger future. That's what makes you a great Chief!"

Laughter erupts from those left in the longhouse and Fisheagle smiles warmly.

"We take your warning and guidance seriously. I would return to Hawk's point. We have new tasks and our traditional tasks. Both must be done through the Winter. I have not been here through the cold season to know what must be done, or how many people can be spared for defense and scouting, which must also be done lest we be caught unawares by another attack. We should have had forewarning, and so should Clearwater and the other villages before they lost almost everything.

"We knew the Grasslanders were coming. Clearwater and the other villages didn't. I do not lay blame, but we must do better. Every life lost, and all of their winter supplies, is a loss to us all. We can support the survivors, but what if it had been a bad year?"

The Chief smiles gently at her. "Thank you, dear Midnight, for laying the trail to a couple of decisions I have come to. First, Hawk, you are now our Chief of Highwater Village. Your mother will arrange for your regalia for significant occasions.

"You will be responsible for everyone in Highwater, their wellbeing and safety first, but also all the ceremonies and representing larger issues to me that you can't resolve, as well as any new issues coming from our alliances. I see that as becoming important in our future."

Fisheagle keeps talking and I mentally catch up. "It seems Fishcamp will still be useful for us, but less so as more changes occur."

Shock focuses my attention. Fishcamp is where we process the food for Winter!

"Some of the People will continue as we were, but others may have new tasks to perform as we adapt to trade with the Song and the new ways we do other things. You, Hawk, are the perfect choice for this. It would have come to you anyway, in time, and you have a good mind for it." He smiles proudly at me.

"Some of you will recall that I had a Second, Dark Otter, who was crushed by a broken tree. I have muddled along without choosing another, but I foresee increased complexity for our People in the near future. You may choose your own Second, but I recommend Seabird."

Seabird sits up straight at the news. Surprise shines in his wide eyes.

"He is social and takes care of what needs doing. Keep him busy and he'll be fine!" Fisheagle finishes with a somewhat evil grin at Seabird, then turns it toward the new Chief of Highwater…me.

Chuckles flutter through the lodge. I may have let my feelings show.

"Seriously, Hawk, you think so hard sometimes about an issue that you become stuck in a think-loop, like a leaf caught in an eddy in the River. That happens to all of us when we deal with complex and important problems. When you feel that happen, ask Seabird what he thinks. Behind his humor lies a talent for cutting to the heart of even weighty matters."

Fisheagle turns to Midnight. "You, dear Midnight, have proven yourself more than once. You took command and wore it well. You are Warleader for our People. We have not had a Warleader for longer than I can remember. Huckleberry, the Keeper of Stories, would know, but it was long ago. I must speak to her anyway. She should be here…"

A woman near the back of the small crowd rises. "Are your eyes getting that bad, Fisheagle? Here I stand!" She waves. "It was nine generations since our last Warleader, who earned the name Bear's-Paw, as the Chief of the day was called Bear and he was the Chief's powerful hand. Do you really think me so old and feeble that I can't tell when our stories are being made? Humph! Not yet!"

Her false displeasure tempered, she says, "Speaking of being old and feeble, I have taken on a young storyteller from the People: one Woodfern, once reckoned by Seabird as being too smart to stick with him and his wandering ways."

Boomer erupts with an enormous guffaw.

"How does she know?!" Seabird asks no one in particular, but he turns and glares suspiciously at me. I do my best to look innocent.

Fisheagle laughs as hard as the rest of us. He fights it down, waits for everyone else to settle, and then goes back to business.

"I remain Chief of all the River People, and I prefer to deal with the other villages to bring them into a working alliance. Messages need to be sent to neighboring communities to expand this thing we are creating. I selected a few helpers I can train to assist me. I know a few devious minds who may be useful. We start down a new trail, more like many new trails, with what we decide over the next year—or years, more like. The Song trader brings transformations to the People's ways when he comes again. I'll be here to help, but each of you is in charge of your own responsibilities. If we do our best, we can face the People confidently, no matter the outcome. You all do your jobs and I'll do mine. The Great Spirit knows what our lives will be like a year from now, but I certainly don't. I have a lot to do, and so do you."

Chapter 36: Midnight Seven Moons On

I eye Nosey, watching him out of the corner of my eye as we walk… More like waddles, in his case. I reckon he has been overly spoiled by the cooks and is definitely putting on weight. For some time I've noticed him working the crowd at meals in the big lodge.

It occurs to me that I've put on a bit of padding myself. The thought that it could mean a child has taken root in my womb flits across my mind. Certainly we have given reason enough for that to happen. A smile starts at my eyes and works its way down. If it's true, all the more reason to stay fit and strong so I can start the child with some of my strength.

I break into a trot as we exit the village. Nosey obligingly speeds up as well. We pass the gate and turn left past the trench. Construction has left a bare, packed skirt of ground all the way around our village. I know what kind of pace Nosey can maintain with his short legs, so I stay at a stride under that. We make two laps around the village hilltop, then I slow to a walk and stop back at the gate. Nosey sits, panting. His tongue lolls back and forth like he's been running all day. He is extremely dramatic at times and clearly he is done.

We settle in the shade of the wall to rest. I feel a crispness in the air and I reflect on the last few months' accomplishments. Boomer and Wei received their enormous cedar-strip ropes, no thanks to me. I told the ladies what was needed, and they did it. I checked in a few times, but they had it well in hand.

We finished the drawbridge over the ditch, which is now filled with rainwater. The Song advisors worked together to make two huge winches with ingenious toothed wheels that let them lock the winches at any point and manage the raising and lowering so the heavy bridge deck can't fall out of control. It still takes three strong men on each winch to raise or lower the deck, but it works. Hawk has an idea for the wall walk that makes perfect sense.

I put Woodshaper and Clayshaper together as a team and they have managed to produce an incredible number of arrow- and spearheads, as sharp and as hard as stone, using the new kilns and the multistep firing process. The two now are called

"Wood" and "Clay," respectively, by everyone, and they are training interested young people in the crafts.

Buckets of arrows sit around the wall walk and the village in protected spots, plus many more are in storage—so well constructed that we already use them as trade goods. They are in high demand with our allies.

Thinking ahead to the cold season, I ordered an enclosure built onto the wall walk all the way around, consisting of a solid back wall, a braced shed roof, and a front half wall of vertical planks about chest high. A couple of cold, wet night shifts convinced me it was necessary, especially when the snow comes. They say the Winters here are extremely variable, with great wet blizzards in some years. In others, snow comes only on the mountains, rain crying from the sky for many moons in the valley. We may have ice storms or merely the torrential rains, sometimes a mix.

I want our warriors to be as effective as we can keep them, so I've instituted a rotating shift with a warm-up break covered by a pool of warriors that wait in the warm longhouse. It requires more bodies, but I believe that a soggy or frozen sentry is not a very good sentry.

Some of the weavers volunteered to make heavy coats for the wall watchers, modeled on Song jackets that are stitched vertically and horizontally to keep the padding from settling. As those are completed, the sentries will be much more comfortable. The thickness will also provide some protection from arrows.

Summer proved to be a good time for diplomacy. Fisheagle sent runners to contact over forty River villages, including Rivergrass, and invited their chiefs to a potlatch. All accepted. None want to suffer the fate of Clearwater and the other villages.

Chapter 37: Hawk Foundations

Each of the chiefs brings a few warriors and some craftsmen to see our fortifications that held back the invaders. The young people are still busy making gifts for all the guests.

Kiapelaneh arrives last with some of his people and Chen and Li, the other two Song advisors, who spend most of their time chattering with Zizhan and Wei. As the delegations arrive, I escort them on tours of the village and its fortifications. The wall alone is impressive, but also the drawbridge with its winches, which the visitors inspect with great interest. When they also see, and examine, the buckets of ready arrows and spears, the expressions I see suggest they are seriously considering an alliance.

After the tour, Fisheagle leads the guests to the lodge for ceremonial greetings, gifts, and feasting. Once we are well fed, the Council of Chiefs begins.

Fisheagle starts by supplying the details of what we know and what actually occurred. He taught me this wise beginning, explaining that secondhand tales are not always so accurate.

Fisheagle's new team of helpers circulate among the crowd of visitors, answering questions and explaining why we've adopted the new ways of doing things, and they tell tales from the Sack of Clearwater and the Battle of Highwater. As I walk by one of our young women, surrounded by a group of guests, I hear her mention the small numbers of our own casualties compared to the number of enemy dead and wounded.

Other Council discussions focus on trade goods for the Song, nudging each Chief to pledge at least half of their trapped furs from this Winter to trade for the new technologies.

Several volunteer that they have deposits of copper in their territories. Others know of sulfur on their lands. Agreements are reached to teach them how to separate the copper from the stone and melt it in the new ovens the Song have now built in both Highwater and Rivergrass.

Coal is brought up at several of the individual conversations I listen in on, as something we will need. When pressed, our negotiator merely says it is better for the new ovens than wood, since it burns hotter and leaves less ash. Kiapelaneh says he has heard of such a thing on the Big Island to the west, across from his territory. He vows to undertake the exploration of trade and alliance.

When the guests depart a few days later, Midnight and I find Fisheagle looking tired, but he wears a pleased smile. I take the spot next to him on the bench as he says, "That was a successful set of negotiations. Never have so many issues been agreed upon by so many chiefs from so many peoples from such a great area!"

I shake my head in admiration and Midnight nods solemn agreement next to me.

Fisheagle's voice is still crisp. "When times are desperate, dare greatly! Things can always turn worse on their own, but they only seem to become better when you really work at it, and sometimes when you hunt deer, a moose appears. Our young men and women carried out most of the negotiations, occasionally checking in with me if unsure how to answer a question. We spent a lot of time in preparation, and they did very well."

Chapter 38: Midnight Spring Conundrums

Winter was peaceful. Still not used to the deep drifts this near the coast, I tended to stick to home or the lodge. One day the wind howled in from the west and it rained and slushed; the next was an outflow of sharp-edged wind and dry snow from the interior mountains howling down the valley on its way to the Sea, leaving great drifts that kept us huddled near fires surrounded by piles of blankets. Hawk organized a weaving group to make more blankets, and we are finally caught up for all the newcomers, and some extras for visitors.

My thought of being with child proves baseless as my cycle continues regularly. I don't know how to feel about it. The idea of bearing and raising a child appeals to me at a gut level, but I also enjoy my responsibilities. Can I be a Warleader with children who need me home to nurse them?

I asked at the women's lodge last moon and Sweetbark, an Elder, explained that River women traditionally foster youngsters when a mother has other obligations, is ill, or dies. It is a welcome task for the good of the community.

Conversely, this war will not last forever. We grow more invincible by the day. We may be faced with a few more battles, but I don't see how the Shaman can keep losing and still have power over the Grassland warriors, not to mention his allies. Many have died for his ambition already, with no slaves and no new territory.

But this day starts as a glorious Spring morning. The rains have stopped for now and the sunlight has real warmth in it. The snow retreats up the mountains daily on either side of the River Valley, much faster on the south wall. In River territory, it would be a full day's walk and a canoe trip from one mountain wall to the other. To the east, the valley narrows into a rugged canyon that begins to rise in elevation past Highwater. Westerly and south, it drops and gradually widens, ending in the wide grassy delta that is Rivergrass territory.

A few northern canyons filled with long lakes and rivers give access into the ranges on our side, but unless you are straight across from them, you can't see them. The north wall has tall rounded tops, still capped by Winter but greening below. The south wall is exactly that, an immense sheer stone barrier with a skirt of talus, thickly treed with maples and hemlock at the base. A couple of even higher mountains soar above. I asked in the women's lodge about them. One is known to emit clouds of smoke.

A short way up, the bright green leafed maples give up, leaving the steep slopes to the dark of the taller evergreens. Gray and whitish scree slides and avalanche runs mar the expanse at irregular intervals. The largest peak on the south side has partly shed its snowy blanket, revealing the image of a frosty white woman with raised wings formed by the cold ridges and warmer rubble slides where the snow has melted. The Elders say she appears almost every Spring, and the People take warning that trouble lurks in the year ahead when she isn't fully formed for at least a few days. Today she appears to have already lost part of a wing.

Watchers on all the trails to the east and south to the River serve as a warning net and, having seen the enemy use teams of two for scouting and ambushes, I have set teams of three to counter them for our trail watches. It's been quiet since the Fall attacks.

The thought stirs the fine hairs on the back of my neck to the sides of my braid. Darting through the gate, I find the Watch Commander on duty. "We are going to have an alert practice, starting right now. Are all the sentry teams out?"

Longarm nods, turns to the alarm team, and hand signs ALERT.

As I climb to the wall walk, the drum begins to thump out the fast beat of warning. I see nothing amiss as I watch the additional teams run out the gate to check on the trail scouts. Nothing further happens for some time. Thinking that at least it has been a good exercise, I spot a wisp of smoke to the southwest. About by the River, I think.

"Southwest, smoke!"

Longarm waves that he heard and shouts a question. "Fishcamp?"

I review the scout positions in my mind. *The enemy shouldn't have been able to sneak a large force through to Fishcamp without one of the teams spotting them, unless it's a small group creating a diversion…*

"I want runners to check all of the sentry points and report back fast!"

Longarm calls to a group of warriors standing ready and relays my instructions. They trot out the gate, circle Highwater, and then sprint for Fishcamp.

The People trickle in to the gate area from all over the village, weapons ready. They fill the open center near the gate and pack all the spaces between the houses. Everyone is armed now—even the children have wicked knives made of the new ceramics. Boomer's been training them in knife fighting using dull wooden knives. Even so, a couple of minor casualties have occurred. They take it seriously and have learned well. They also train with smaller bows, and many are very good shots. They face slavery, or possibly worse, if they're captured by Shaman's fighters, so our last line of defense learns to survive—or at least to hurt their attackers—while clustered in the open center of the village.

I scan the village and check if any vulnerabilities jump out, but the People look ready. I toy with the idea of a possible distraction, to draw us out. If that is the case, a very large force is somewhere. Grasslanders have beaten themselves bloody against our defenses twice now, and any sane person would not attack again unless they thought they had some advantage.

I consider other possibilities. After the potlatch, most of the other River villages have built their own village walls modeled on Highwater. Almost all should be finished by now.

No, diversion is the only thing that makes sense. They are trying to draw our warriors out of the village's fortifications.

The tactic suggests that a lot of them are nearby to threaten us. In their place, one plan might be to draw out as many as possible, slaughter us, and then attack the walls with fire to make an entry point. Let the flames eat a hole, or at least a weak spot. The walls are thick tree trunks, though, so that would take quite a bit of time… *Ladders?*

"Send more warriors to the wall! We need poles to push off ladders! Longarm, send runners to the teams. They are to avoid initial contact with the enemy. Have them pull back into cover until they can see what the attack looks like, and bring me some reports! Then they are to strike and run. Harass them! Their job is to keep the enemy off balance and not end up dead!"

He waves and I see him send the runners. We will have a strong force outside as well as in. I keep working the situation over in my mind, trying to see any other preparations I can make to help our troops survive. I worry that I have split my forces, but the wall should make that all right. The heavy gray smoke that rises from Fishcamp suggests it is gone, or will be. Word of that has circulated and I can see on their wrathful faces that the People are ready to fight. A buzz like a swarm of angry bees sizzles from the armed crowd inside. Longarm and his men keep them from flowing like the River in snowmelt into the enemy forces.

I have some handpicked agents with the troops. If anything goes sideways, they are to pull back and report. One dashes in and climbs straight up the ladder to me.

"Yes, they torched Fishcamp. We estimate almost a hundred. We couldn't sneak close enough to hear anything useful, except that another force is somewhere. They don't seem nearly as organized, or as trained, as we are." He nods in respect to me. "They have no sentries out and as we watched, they milled around, perhaps waiting for something. We saw no strangers on the way back. If more are in our territory, they must be somewhere else."

Thanking him, I send him back with instructions to scout around the village at a distance in small teams.

"We have to find the main force, but have one team keep an eye on the pond scum who burned Fishcamp. They will probably join up with the main force. You may be able to follow them."

Scowling in frustration, I worry about that main force. *No reports of them so far. Where are they?* Almost in answer, our scouts begin to pour out of the woods and through the gate. Seeing the numbers, I run to meet them. As I swing onto the ladder, three scouts who had started up reverse and slide back down. On the ground, I spin to meet them.

"What have you seen?"

"They advance in an arc around the village. Several of our scouts are dead. We hoped to work around them, but so many…" He trails off and looks at me intensely. "Three, maybe four or five hundred."

The number registers as a cold knot growing in my gut. "Go back out there! Use the back door if you have to. I want runners to all of the villages within a day's march. Tell them we need them, and tell them why. Be careful! A few of the enemy aren't worth the message not getting through."

Nodding, he turns on his heel, calls the other scouts together, and passes the orders. The teams race out the gate as they learn their assignments, spreading apart like the sun's rays on misty days as they gain some distance.

This is our one small chance to call for help.

David Oliver-Godric

Chapter 39: Narrator
Chawathil

A scout team found a canoe that hadn't been burned near the remains of Fishcamp, which still sent twisty trails of smoke skyward. They launched it into the River to carry the news of the battle coming to Highwater, rowing upstream to Xwelich, Skawalook, and Chawathil. It was a hard row with the Spring freshet still running high and strong.

Chawathil was burning.

The three warriors pulled the canoe onto a landing and spread out, weapons ready, cautiously working their way up the bank. Once over the high-water cut, a large flat meadow with scattered groves of trees lay between them and the village—or what was left of it. Wisps of smoke trampled their hopes.

They spread out even farther. Screech-Owl went upriver before turning inland, running from tree to tree. Lynx went straight in, low in the tall grass. His was the shortest track, so he crawled as close as he dared if any enemy sentries remained, and waited for the others to settle in position. Kestrel angled downriver before turning inland.

Chawathil had only started building their wall, and no ditch was begun around the village either. As the warriors got closer, they saw that the houses and the longhouse had been burning for a while. Lynx noted burned arrows, with remains of charred cloth wrapped behind the heads, sticking out of the structures. They worked their way toward the center of the village, finding some bodies—mostly men. Nothing else moved except the smoke and a soft breeze stirring the grass. Silence told the tale.

The three met by the still-burning longhouse. Lynx shook his head. "The Chief was warned—this village was on the main path to Highwater from the Grasslands! We search for survivors, then check Lukseetsissum and Skawalook." The others nodded and split up, making a fast search of the area. All they found were more bodies.

The other two villages were the same as Chawathil and, although their walls were farther along, they still weren't complete. Kestrel shared his thoughts: "I think the villagers are being held somewhere until the raiders have grabbed as much territory as they can. Then they will be put to work rebuilding. Any of our villages left between Lukseetsissum and Highwater are probably gone, so I suggest we head for home and try to report. We can do nothing here."

The journey back was downstream and passed quickly with the freshet driving to the Sea. They hid the canoe upriver from Fishcamp, and a short time later crawled under the wall through Hawk's hidden entry and looked for Midnight. They found her still on the wall walk. Following their report, she sent them to find Hawk and brief him as well.

Grassland warriors arrived and spread around the wall, staying a little beyond reach of Highwater's bows. A few defenders took long shots anyway, and a fewer number of Grasslanders dropped. The enemy milled around a bit, but mostly stayed out of range of any but the best archers.

Chapter 40: Midnight
The Second Battle of Highwater

The incoming arrows are still few, so I poke my head up for a quick scan. Teams push their way through the enemy mob, carrying armloads of wood. They make piles spaced along the front line. A shaft comes whizzing toward my head and I duck. With a solid *thunk,* I see it hit the wall behind me and stick.

"Otter, see if they are doing that all around the village."

Otter makes the circuit and confirms they are.

"Tell Hawk to prepare the inside teams to fight fires." I know what is coming from the scout reports on Chawathil and the other villages.

The Grasslanders light the woodpiles. A cloud of smoke rises all around Highwater, obscuring the enemy just as fire arrows start to arc over into the village. Most land on dirt, but a few stick into the wall and buildings, and some into People. Hawk's fire crews use buckets to scoop dust and dirt up to throw on the fire arrows and whatever they hit. This goes on for a while.

The Grasslanders creep furtively through the thickening smoke, piling green branches on the fires. The tactic effectively masks the enemy, also making it harder for us to see the incoming arrows. It works, but a sudden breeze strengthens—an outflow of dense cold air from the still-frozen high mountains upstream—and the heavy gusts fall into and fill the lower valley, pushing the smoke downstream toward Rivergrass. Billows sweep along and for some moments we can see, then an eddy whips a cloud between us. In the midst of one of the billows, I see glows appear. Fire arrows! Some strike inside the village.

The enemy pushes closer under the smoke covering and starts arcing fire arrows to drop onto our roofs, like a huge swarm of flaming osprey swooping in from all directions. Some of the archers are trying to take out the wall watch. The vast numbers of arrows mean that some are finding their marks. We're forced to crouch below the half wall, unable to return fire with any accuracy.

Frustrated, I seethe as my mind searches for a solution. *A mass of the enemy is right in front of my archers. If we could fire back without exposing ourselves…*

I stare at the boards in front of me and an idea tickles my thoughts. The half wall is made of short planks fastened from the outside.

"Kick out every fifth wall board! Stay to the side of the openings to fire. Pass the word!" So saying, I kick out the plank to my right. Arrows might find their way in, but at least we can see to return fire now. An eager enemy archer spots the new opening and his arrow flies straight through the gap and sticks in the back weather wall.

We lose a few watchers whose timing is unfortunate or who don't dodge back fast enough, but now two archers can fire across each other's line of sight under cover at each open gap. I pass an order that anyone not shooting will— carefully!—gather the enemy arrows from the back wall. Some don't stick when they hit at an angle and simply fall onto the walk. Those are collected and fired right back at the enemy.

Smiling at the thought that we are killing the enemy with their own arrows, I see a clear eddy open and shoot another Grasslander in the little hollow at the base of the throat as he draws his bow.

At this point, the wall watch has a wealth of targets. We really don't have to aim, even when we can see. A sea of Grasslander warriors is in our firing windows. Our own casualties have dropped to an occasional lucky shot from the enemy. Young people carry injured or killed warriors down to Greatheart and his team. Longarm sends up a new warrior to replace every one who comes down. Whoever is in charge of the Grasslander army isn't a creative thinker, but he does seem determined.

Chapter 41: Longbow Spirits

As a Grassland Commander, the enemy adapts to every trick I've come up with. The spirits of this place take their side against us, blowing our smoke cover downriver, away from the battle. I call to the spirits of our People to do *something* to help us in this maelstrom. We shoot at the openings in the palisade, and nothing happens. We shoot fire arrows into the village, and all we see are some wisps of smoke pushed away by the outflow winds.

We need ladders, but that's not going to happen in time.

I wish I'd thought of that beforehand.

What can we do?

Chapter 42: Midnight Bloodstink

The carnage goes on for hours. Without ladders, the enemy's arrows aren't hitting anything but the back of the weather shield and the front of the half wall.

A young girl reaches around through a firing gap to retrieve an arrow stuck right on the outside. Before I can pull her back, an arrow buries itself in her shoulder. Leaping for her leg as she topples out, I wrap one hand around her ankle. The shock of her weight jerks us into a slide. Desperation strengthens my grip and I twist so one sliding knee hits the wall and manage to stop her fall. I slap my other hand on her leg and barely manage to drag her back before another arrow can take her life. Her eyes still wide with pain and fear, she offers me a weak smile and reaches out a hand, just brushing my fingertips as she passes me in the arms of a crouching warrior who carries her to the ladder and down to the healers.

Bodies pile up outside as the advantage of height turns the battle in our favor. I make a mental note to reward the Song advisors, somehow, when this is over. In time, the enemy dead number enough for the survivors to hide behind them. Some start to roll and drag corpses into barriers. Still the slaughter continues all around the wall, but the casualties grow fewer as more hide behind their own dead. My archers begin to fire almost straight up so our arrows drop in on the raiders. It's tricky to hit a specific target, but we have lots of arrows.

Many of the arrows stuck in the back wall are bloody, and some are tipped with our ceramic heads, so they are scavenging ammunition. The return fire slows, gradually tapering off. By nightfall, the enemy seems to have lost interest, since only an occasional arrow lofts into the village or whacks into the wall.

Spent, like all of my warriors, I order every fourth warrior to take a dinner break while I do a crouching run around the walk. It's the same everywhere. By this time, arrows have stopped falling completely. I see enemy cookfires in the distance, well outside of bowshot, and decide I can take a break myself. I call to Nighthawk, one of my lieutenants, to take charge of the defense, such as it is, and climb carefully down the ladder and point myself at the longhouse.

My head feels like a fog has settled onto it, and that short walk seems to take forever. Finally I plop down on a bench and stare at a story pole. Someone brings a plate of food and a cup of water and places it in front of me. I sense time passing, but I'm too tired to move. After some time, I summon the will to take a long drink.

Someone sits next to me and a hand caresses my shoulder. Turning toward the hand, I recognize Hawk. His face penetrates the fog and releases me from the bonds of exhaustion. Throwing my arms around him and holding him tight is good. After a bit, I start crying into his shoulder.

"The arrow girl… I almost lost her!"

Hawk wraps his arms around me and hugs me while I sob. Something furry rubs against my legs and Nosey pounces onto my lap. He doesn't like ladders, so he hasn't seen me all day, but he's sensitive to people's moods and surely senses the distress in the air. He has missed me, not understanding. Now he snuggles close.

***

Dawn finds me back on the wall, refreshed and angry with myself. I should have organized a surprise counterattack in the night to finish the enemy while they were hurt and discouraged, but I was so tired. I look out at the ring of bodies piled high and wide, stretching as far as I can see around the wall, and I shriek loud and long. All of the fear and horror of the previous day is in that scream, along with the heartbreaking loss of friends and family, and for the potential of every single soul who passed yesterday.

No sign of attackers remain, only wisps of smoke from their fires of the night before. I register that fact and climb down the ladder to find Hawk.

"I think they may have gone."

He looks at me with surprise, then his brow furrows. "We need to find them."

I nod. "I'll send scouts—first to check their camps, then to locate them and hold the trail. They're somewhere. I don't believe they've given up and gone home, and even if they have, we must find their captives and free them. This isn't over for me."

I look sadly into his eyes. "You will have to organize the burials. Keep reminding yourself, and those on the burial parties, that it was them or us. They brought this to us, and they would have killed or enslaved us all. Keep our People angry so they don't fall into a chasm of grief."

Pausing, I think about the lost friends and family in the other villages. "I will do my best to find our People and retrieve them. Then we'll need to send advisors to the destroyed villages to make sure they finish their fortifications. They should have been as ready as we were. They had time."

Hawk, pale, nods. "Yes, they should have been. You are going after them." His eyes start sad, then turn cold and hard. "I wonder how many other communities waited too long…"

"Hawk, I have to pull about fifty of the best warriors out of Highwater for the rescue. That is a good number for a fast, effective force. It's large enough to hit hard, and small enough to be speedy and flexible. You will need to be ready for harassing actions by the invaders. I don't believe they will attempt another major attack—they'll try to take the wounded and the captives they have back to the Grasslands. Make a good count on their dead. I want to know how many of them we killed. They don't seem concerned about taking them home. Count the firepits from when they pulled back."

I grab him in a hug, which he gives back. It lasts a long time.

I whisper, "This must never happen again."

Hawk nods into my neck, pulls himself up and away. "We survived it pretty well, thanks to your devious mind. You were a step ahead of them all the way."

"We all did this. Every one of us stepped up and accomplished what was demanded by circumstances. I have enormous pride for our People. You tell them that when I leave."

Hawk nods, sad-faced. "We both have work to do. Let's get it done."

I smile and hope the love in my eyes shines through, then stand to go to pick my team. Bloodstink still hangs in the air like a cold fog.

Chapter 43: Midnight Search and Rescue

Before I leave, Hawk orders teams of nine to each village in the area. Their instructions are to carry the news of what happened to the three communities that were destroyed, find out how far along the defenses in each surviving settlement are, and prod them into action if they aren't well along. He also sends teams of three to farther communities, including canoes to Rivergrass and other villages on the north side of the River, to spread the news and to reassure our allies that we survived a major attack.

I order my team to have a day of rest—no wall watches. The next morning, while giving Nosey a cuddle, I try to explain. "I have to be gone for a while and I can't take you with me. You watch out for Hawk. He will give you cuddles—just not as good as I do."

Nosey snuggles close, pushing at my hand with his bristly nose, looking up with his bright eyes right into mine. I cuddle him back, and then regretfully rise and walk away. I send runners for fifty of my most trusted people—mostly veterans of the previous trips up the trail and back, and those who distinguished themselves on the wall—telling them to gather at the longhouse. While I wait, I have a solid breakfast, shared with Nosey, of course. They trickle in and finally I begin my briefing.

"We have a job to do. At least three villages were raided for slaves. I want them back!"

The team rumbles, low and menacing. They are in no mood for failure, as most of them had relatives and friends in those villages.

"Badger is my Second on this mission. Boomer is needed here if another attack comes. Possibly a thousand of those butchers remain and we know the trail they will take. They have a day's head start, but they won't move very fast with all those prisoners, some of whom are children and elderly, so we have a chance to intercept. We don't know if the enemy is all together, or if the main force is headed somewhere else to strike, leaving a smaller guard force. Some of you are good trackers. We need your eyes on the ground and reading signs. That will tell us much. Have your last good meal for a while and pack lightly for a long run. Meet me at the gate when the sun is at its high point."

***

"Find them! Trackers, front and spread out. Don't miss anything. Let's go!" I lead my team to the blazed trail and call out two hunters. "You two go downriver a short way. Look for signs, then turn around and catch back up with us as you can. I want to make sure they didn't split up here."

They nod and take off. I start following the blazes upriver. Remembering the Grasslanders' ambush tactics, I send a team of three to each side of the trail, giving them time to gain some distance ahead of our main party. A short time later, I feel more secure and lead the main group on again.

Not much farther on, the two downriver trackers catch up. They report seeing no fresh signs on the downriver trail.

Satisfied that we aren't leaving some of the enemy behind us, we push on. Three trackers are on point ahead of the main group. One stops and waits for me to catch up.

"We are seeing indications of a large group passing this way. We can't tell if it is all of them or not."

I nod and he runs to catch his team. I feel better that we are on the trail of some of the enemy, at least. I really hope this bunch has the prisoners.

We push as hard as we can to catch up. The lead scouts report the tracks are fresher as the sun moves west. It's almost dusk, but still nothing is in sight. I call a meal break, sending runners for the point men and the wings.

It's bannock, dried berries, and smoked meat: packed with nutrition to keep us going as long as we have to. Each warrior has selected their own supplies, knowing that we won't have any fires on this mission, at least until we have the final prisoners. Between the food and the rest, we feel fresher when finished, so I suggest we carry on through the night. No one grumbles. They all want to have their friends and families back.

Now I pull the wings in, since they would not be able to keep up, and we remove our moccasins to feel the trail with our feet in the opaque darkness. Hopefully any watchers will miss us passing. Experienced hunters, we move silently at all times. Dark forces with a dark purpose, we have actually picked up the pace on the night run as our other senses rise to dominance.

David Oliver-Godric

Chapter 44: Midnight
First Ambush

The sky lightens as the sun peeks above the rim of the world behind the mountains to the east, and we are still running. As I open my mouth to call a break for food and rest, one of the point runners drops back to me. He whispers, "Smoke smell."

I wave him back to point and signal HALT AND GATHER as one of the wing men appears out of the brush with a young girl right behind him. She runs to me as I kneel, her arms wrap around my neck and she sobs away her fear and breathes a fierce "Midnight!" into my ear. It seems everyone from the area knows about the tall Warleader who came from the Grasslands to fight against the raiders.

I put a finger to her lips, smile, and whisper with her for a short time, telling her she'll be safe. Beckoning to the scout who found her, I hand her back to him and point south behind us. They move off the trail, hiding in the dark forest undergrowth.

We continue forward, setting the pace we have run all night, fast and silent. A short way on, I smell the smoke and gather the main force in. Pointing to Badger, I crook my fingers to bring him to me.

"Take half the force and work around to the north of the trail. Spread your people in an arc around that side of the camp. Then send a runner to report what you can see. When you hear or see us move, take the sentries first, as silently as possible, and then kill as many as fast as you can."

He nods and efficiently sorts out his half of the warriors. After they vanish into the brush, I lead the rest to the south of the trail and work forward. As I expected, the camp is on the north side of the trail. The runner arrives and reports about fifty enemy, with perhaps twice that many captives. I tap UNDERSTOOD on his arm and silently spread my team in an arc around the southwest of the camp. After a quick check that everyone's ready, I lead them in.

***

The quietest way to kill something is to cut its throat, fast and deep. It's a trick I learned from watching cougars hunt—from a safe vantage point, of course. All of the sentries, and many of the enemy, die that way in the first minutes. Some wake in time to see death coming, then some rouse in time to scream. After that, they die scrabbling for their weapons. Others try to strike as they die. The last few fight for their lives. Two surrender.

With the enemy bodies stripped of anything useful, I have the rescued prisoners make up packs of salvage. I briefly interrogate them for new information. I learn that they were sent back in groups from each of the communities that were pillaged, and several groups are ahead of them. They are all about the same size, both in warriors and in captives.

The two captives either don't know or aren't telling where the main force has gone. I order their hands tied and assign two warriors to watch them. Before we leave, we make sure we haven't left anything for Grasslander scouts except bodies.

I feel both elated and distraught at thinking we need more warriors. We can take two or three more camps the same way, but each action costs us more losses as guards for prisoners, and our luck could run out at any time. Coming up behind the enemy, they receive no warning, but if some of the groups have significantly more warriors and we do take casualties, our force will dwindle quickly. Some of the enemy are bound to be lucky—a few might even be smart, but I haven't seen signs of that yet.

My force is exhaustedly jubilant at our success, but we are tired to the bone after the long run and then the fight. I order everyone, except for two sentries, to sleep. The guards will pick replacements. We rest for half a day, then go on.

Badger comes to me. "You will sleep for the full half day. Don't argue. We need you sharp."

I start to argue, then quit. I know he's right.

***

Badger shakes me awake. I eat and pack my gear. Everyone else has already done the same and they're ready.

Badger has armed some of the rescued people with enemy weapons, mostly bows, arrows, and knives, except the young children. Leafhopper, one of our warriors, will guide them the two days' march to Highwater. The party can hunt and forage for food. We found some captured supplies, but not a lot—certainly not enough for even the Grasslanders to sustain themselves for the journey home. I make a mental note of the fact. At some point, hunger will slow the other enemy groups.

We are off down the trail again, hunting Grasslanders. That idea no longer holds discomfort for me.

Chapter 45: Hawk
Bloody Ground

While my body is on the wall scanning for trouble, my mind lingers on Midnight. I focus as people appear from the lush Spring greenery and draw near the gate. I call down to Longarm, "People coming in!"

Guards move to either side of the gate, weapons ready. Running for the ladder, I barely touch the rungs on the way down. First in, Leafhopper walks straight to us.

His face splits in as gleeful a grin as I've ever seen. "Midnight sends the first of several gifts! We found these people in a camp about two days up the blaze trail. We had to put down about a hundred Grasslanders, but it only took a few minutes." Still grinning, he waits for my reaction, sharing his glee with the sky. He continues on, relaying—in bloody detail—the story of the attack and the intelligence they got out of the captives.

Longarm steps in and grabs both prisoners by the neck. "I'll take these two!" After dragging them around, he passes them to a couple of warriors standing nearby. "Tie them to posts in the longhouse…for now." The two captives' faces fade to a bloodless white.

Watching the stream of people still coming in through the gate, I realize I'll have to find food and lodging for them, and this will most likely only be the first batch. If Midnight's intelligence is correct, up to 400 more may arrive within the next week or so! Their villages are destroyed—I have to work it out fast.

I climb the ladder to the wall again to clear my mind. My first thought is that Midnight might need more help. I have a bunch of new warriors, so that frees some of my Highwater troops to help Midnight.

Leaning out, I call down to Longarm, who looks up.

"Organize about fifty fresh warriors ready to reinforce Midnight. She's at least four days ahead, so send them out soonest!"

Longarm points to one of his seconds, who runs off to take care of it.

Chapter 46: Midnight Execute!

We spot the second group of captives and retreating Grasslanders a day farther up the trail, about sundown. Again, the northerners camp on the north side of the trail. I pass the word to execute exactly as before, figuring that you don't change what works. My team settles in well short of the enemy camp and takes the opportunity for rotating sleep and meal times. It's cold rations again.

After a while, I switch the scouts watching the enemy camp. The first set of scouts is relieved as darkness settles in. Coyote reports what they have seen.

"They treat the prisoners worse than dogs. The captives are all tired and hungry, but they eat in front of them and give them nothing. I saw warriors kicking children and adults out of their way. One beat a man who begged for food for his children."

I put a hand on his arm. "We will put an end to this tonight."

A scream echoes from the enemy camp.

Rage rises, but Coyote grabs my shoulder. "No. We will end it tonight. Too many of ours will die if we attack now, and more of these parties lie ahead."

The fire inside me dies to a smolder. Nodding, I force myself to calm, and finally let out a deep breath. "We can't bring back the dead, but we can bring back the living." Clapping my hand on his shoulder and giving it a squeeze, I sit and wait.

Time passes slowly for everyone. Darkness descends; activity in the camp slows. This bunch has been on the trail longer, so no doubt they are tired. After what seems like an eternity, the scouts report that everyone is bedding down. Now we wait until they are all in a deep sleep.

The rumble of snores is the signal for action. I have my best warriors tasked to take out the few Grassland sentries first, then the rest of the two teams will ease into place for the attack. I still wait. Finally, I give the sign to my southern team. They move in, and the northern team moves in as well.

The sentries die first, with no alarm. Then it is simply "Work fast and move on to the next." My team is a practiced killing machine at this point. We suffer a few minor injuries and this time we take no captives. Once again, the freed prisoners swarm us with thanks.

***

We divide the rations and weapons immediately, building up the fires so we can see to work. Then I instruct the refugee party to head back along the trail with the wounded, and one warrior for escort.

My troops are still wound up and fairly well rested, so I lead them off down the trail to the next killing ground. It is more than that, though. It is also a mission of mercy, and before we go, I remind them of it. I don't want them to dwell on the killing—that will eat at the soul.

I feel it myself. Some part of my spirit has changed since I threw stones at the Shaman—may evil spirits torment him in his darkest dreams—and this mission has pushed the evolution farther from the innocent whom I still recall. May I never lose her entirely.

Over the next few days, we repeat the process twice more. I estimate we have killed over 500 of the enemy, captured fifteen, and rescued about 1,600 of the People. The last group says at least one more group is ahead. I sigh when I hear that. We are all ready for this to end, but the rescuing is food for the soul. To think all those people would have been lost to a life of slavery. It's abhorrent, unacceptable, intolerable.

That keeps us all going.

Chapter 47: Midnight Grayrabbit

The reinforcements arrive and I want to hug them all. I satisfy myself with the undulating song of victory. As a bold song of contempt for our enemies, all the warriors join in. Those who have been with me from the start drown out the newcomers, who don't know—yet—the cost of that howl of defiance. Their shocked faces tell us veterans that we are at another level of being, of feeling. No joy lives in that emotion, a mixture of horror and fulfillment. We have earned that cry, and we own it.

I declare a day off. "We will take a break—eat and rest some more. Then we will hunt those evil spawn of the Grasslands and teach them what it means to attack The People of The River!"

So we eat and sleep, and stories are told. The newcomers are appalled by the tales, but they know they would have done the same, and their time comes in the next few days. Some of the older warriors shudder at the stories. They know they can do what has to be done, and will when the time comes. Some of the young, inexperienced ones are eager.

In the morning, refreshed and reinforced, we run the trail again. I have a twinge of regret at the lost time, but I know it was worth it since we make better time than the previous two runs. The veterans are refreshed, and the energy of the new troops has been restored after their long run from Highwater.

About midday, we are all surprised when scouts come back with word of a large force with prisoners ahead. The scouts estimate close to sixty of the enemy, with about thirty prisoners. I guess this is the group who hit Chawathil, given the larger numbers of the enemy. It's not smart to think this battle will be a repeat of the smaller groups. The element of surprise is a multiplier of our strength.

All right. So what can we do? How can we gain more advantage? My frown slowly turns from worry to a dark smile. The enemy is my greatest asset.

We set up as we have before. When the enemy is sound asleep, we go in hard and fast. It is the usual butcher's work, except for the few who awaken fully and jump up, weapons ready.

I light an arrow from one of their fires, send it straight up into the air, and we all turn and vanish into the darkness. The glare of the fire still in my eyes, I trip on a deadfall, but catch myself and keep going.

We rendezvous at two centers, one up trail and one down. Badger has the up-trail team. We pull back, well out of sight, and watch the chaos in the enemy camp from the darkness of the forest.

It's interesting how fear can take hold when you can't see your enemy. We could be anywhere. Within a very short time, the enemy has killed about thirty of their own out of surprise and sheer terror. A figure appears and runs silently toward you out of the dark. You kill it! If you realize your mistake, what can you do? Another figure is coming at you, screaming for your blood…

I hold my people quiet in the darkness. The enemy numbers have dropped to about twenty-five. The idiots don't even have the sense to trample out their fires. Judging the chaos sufficient, I scream like an eagle and both of my teams attack.

The Grasslanders are completely demoralized with two attacking fronts from opposite sides. Heads swing one way, then the other. They can't tell how many we are. A few drop their weapons and kneel, then a few more, then the last.

I order the enemy secured with ropes, then we link them together with more rope, all of it removed from the ex-prisoners. Leaving a strong guard on them, I turn to the newly freed River People. Some I know, others are simply grateful. I reassure them all that they are safe.

When the chaos settles down, I address them. "Do any of you know if more prisoners are down the trail ahead of you?"

No one speaks up right away. They talk among each other. Finally, one woman comes forward, blood still on her wrists from her bondage. A recent knife cut crosses her nose from her forehead and marks her cheek. "We don't know for sure, but we don't think so. The newest tracks all pointed towards home."

I thank them. Relief washes over me like a cool, clean shower. I turn to the Grassland prisoners and ask them the same question, allowing shades of threat to creep into my tone. They all deny any more groups lie ahead.

***

I sense one of them, a very young warrior, might have more to say. I stalk across to him, seize him by the arm, and drag him with me, away from the others. Badger wanders over and stands nearby, keeping his eyes on the young man.

"Truth. That's what I want from you." I grasp him by both arms and pull him in until his face is inches from mine. "Tell me the whole story."

The young man nods, eyes wide and shadowed with fear.

I glance at Badger. "Make sure we are not disturbed." He signs AGREE and I pull the captive away from the camp, Badger trailing at a discreet distance, and find a downed tree we can sit on where we are screened from the camp. I seat myself on the log, motioning for him to sit next to me. "What's your name, son?"

"Grayrabbit. You're Midnight, aren't you." It is more a statement than a question.

I nod. "Do you know why I left?" He signs NO. "I saw the Shaman kill the Chief so he could start this war. I shamed him in front of the village. He would have killed me—or had me killed, more like."

Grayrabbit's face pales. "That's not what we were told! Shaman said you killed the Chief in his house and started a fire to cover it up. Shaman dragged him out, but it was too late."

I shake my head. "*He* killed the Chief and started the fire. I found the Chief as he laid dying. That's why I screamed at Shaman." Belief grows in his eyes. "You know all the people who left? They came with me to the River People, to be safe. You can talk to them."

I let him turn that over in his mind. It takes him some time to work through the implications of what he has heard. I can almost read his thoughts by the changes of expression in his eyes. Finally, I see decision.

"Shaman convinced all of the surrounding villages, our allies and trade partners, to join us. He split us into a large group that followed the blazed trail, and I came with a smaller force. We followed the River, even though it is hard going. No one knows the trails over the mountains. When we got to where the land opens out, we started to hit the villages. The first ones were small and surrendered when they saw the number of our warriors. We kept on until we had this bunch here. The last two villages had started to build walls. They fought, but we were too many and they didn't resist long. Our orders were to return back home with the slaves and loot. That's really all I know. The main force came down this trail."

The cold calculation of the Shaman sickens me. I don't know what twisted the wretch, but any mad animal needs to be put down for the safety of the People. Anyway, it seems we do have the last group of prisoners. I still don't know where the main force—or what's left of it—went, but we've accomplished our mission. It is time to go home. I study Grayrabbit for a minute.

"They will know you told me something. If I put you with the rest of the prisoners, they will likely try to kill you at the first chance. I can't simply let you go, for several reasons."

I look him in the eyes. He is thoroughly miserable. "Because you are so young, I will give you a choice, which is more than your Shaman or your comrades would." I see his eyes brighten a tiny bit with a seedling of hope. "I will take your word that you will not try to escape, nor will you do anything to harm any of my people, or our mission. Do you swear by your ancestors?"

"I swear by my ancestors that I will not try to escape, and I will not harm any of your people or your mission." He lets out a huge sigh. "I didn't like what we were doing."

I nod solemnly. "Good! Come on, then, you will be my helper. Stay close. Some of my people will not be happy about this either."

We rise and walk back to the camp. Grayrabbit follows a step or two behind. Badger ambles along in the rear like the great bear that he is, with a quirk to his lip that might be half a smile.

I check that the troop is in order and we set out on the trail home.

Chapter 48: Hawk
Missing Links

Nosey snuggles up next to me on the bench in the longhouse. He's followed me everywhere except the wall walk since Midnight left. He sleeps a lot and isn't his previous perky self. We both miss her.

Most of the longhouse was converted into living space for the refugees, but the front quarter is still a communal dining area and meeting place. I consider what I can do with the refugees for the longer term. We really don't have room for an extra 160 people, and a fast runner has brought word that Midnight is on her way home with 600 more, plus the 100 warriors who are with her, though they already have houses.

Another thing nags at me. Midnight reports killing about 600. I chuckle at that number—she did most of it with fifty warriors!—and I have ordered a count of the bodies from the second battle at Highwater. My people report 337 Grasslander bodies. But the scouts estimated 300–500 enemy at the beginning of the attack. Midnight's tally would not have been a part of that. They were a separate group who came down the River route. So 60–260 unaccounted-for Grasslanders may be somewhere. I tend to think the top estimate is a result of overestimating, and the lowest of underestimating. That still leaves 100–150 nasty characters wandering around somewhere, possibly looking for trouble. Our count of campfires after the battle suggests 60–100 survived, some of those wounded. We found blood around most of the campfires. The enemy would have bound their wounds before leaving.

Our refugee problem has a couple of solutions. One, we can send resources and craftsmen to rebuild the wrecked villages. Midnight's rescued people who fled oppression can work as well. But…the missing Grasslanders wandering around somewhere worries me. I still have to defend Highwater from a possible attack, and we must also be prepared to defend the rebuilding efforts in other villages against a major force.

I stare at the table some more. It isn't helping. My head pops upright when I remember that I have a labor force that can make short work of almost any project and provide security for it. Not far away, another plateau-like defensible hill would be perfect to build a new fortress on. A family of cougars lives in the meadows and brush, so we will have to be alert when we move in, but they don't like bear scent, and I know someone who has two bladders of bear urine. If we sprinkle it around the perimeter, we can encourage the cougars to move on—hopefully not around Highwater. That would give us two fortresses able to support each other in a battle, and also house the refugees until the villages can be rebuilt.

The other option is to send a large workforce to Skawalook when Midnight's force returns—she is probably a day or two out by now. Her troops can rest and recuperate at Highwater. Skawalook had a good part of their wall up already, but not enough when the attack came. It shouldn't take very long to finish, and then it will be secure and living quarters can be built. The more I think about it, the more it seems like a workable idea. I reach down to Nosey and scratch his head. Jumping up, I walk out, heading to see Fisheagle first, to brief him on my plan. Nosey pads along with me. I know he's lonely.

So am I.

***

Midnight's team and the refugees arrive the next day. She leads the way through the gate and I run to meet her, wrap her in my arms for a long kiss, then whirl her around and hug her some more. I stroke her beautiful long hair and she looks at me with her heart in her eyes. She grins from ear to ear as Nosey rubs against our legs. He was so unhappy the whole time she was gone, even losing some of his roundness. When people offered him treats, he mostly drooped his head and wandered off. It was almost like the treats reminded him of Midnight, and he didn't have the heart for it.

Now she bends down and scoops him up for a good bear hug and a cuddle. When she puts him down, he bounces around, rubbing against her legs, then mine. We share another kiss, and Midnight's victory cry rises from the gathering crowd—a hero's welcome. Families are finding relatives they thought were lost forever. The People she has rescued keep coming through the gate to cheer after cheer. Tears of joy flow like Spring streams. A crowd forms around Midnight, thankful relatives reaching out to touch her in thanks. I step back to avoid being trampled by the mob. I see Nosey scooting away for the same reason and gather him up in my arms. We share the joy of her return and the hazards of it as well.

The crowd dwindles as relatives take their family members to wherever they are staying, or to the longhouse for a real meal. I realize I've been overthinking again. Most of the refugees have family here, and they can share houses!

The longhouse fills up quickly and waiting lines form. The cooks send people out to eat their meals elsewhere so they can serve the next batch. All the cooks are working now, but it still takes time to feed everyone. No one is angry or impatient. We all have too much to be thankful for. The celebration will likely go on for hours into the night.

Meanwhile, the prisoners are taken to a new structure I ordered built over the Winter: a solidly made prison. I anticipated the need, and it is now full. The prisoners are fed as well…eventually.

The prisoners unanimously chose slavery over execution and I offered to take them to work at Skawalook. Close to 100 refugees, from various villages, will be available to help with rebuilding. Zizhan and Wei can help with any technical issues. We have the resources, now we have to do it as fast as possible. Boomer is in charge, and the workers all have their weapons handy. We aren't taking any chances with the slaves, or any wandering Grasslander war parties.

Chapter 49: Shaman
The Costs of War

A procession of failure marches into my village—beaten hunters returning without slaves *or* plunder. I refuse to call them warriors. I see no goods, no prisoners, and far fewer of them remain for another invasion.

Longbow, the fool who led them, walks toward me.

"What has happened? Where are my slaves?"

His eyes tell me the truth. I sense his spirit squirming like a worm in muddy water.

"Don't tell me you failed again! Aaaah!"

Why can't the clod accomplish this one simple task? I gave him the honor of leading, not once, but several times!

"You are useless! Where is the plunder? The slaves? What have you done?" I beat the ground with my feet, lost in a dark cloud of rage. The pustule dares to look angry.

He goads me with a pointless reply. "You are Shaman, tasked with communing with the spirits for the benefit of your people. Instead, you value things over the many lives of our People who have died for your plan. I had misgivings about your motives from the time you came up with this disastrous idea. Do you even know how many of our People are lost to us? Do you understand that none of the other bands who came to help us will even trade with us again? It sickens me that the Elders will tell my name next to yours forever." He spits on the ground at my feet.

Too angry to respond, I feel the vision of living in a lush garden of food turn to sand flowing through my fingers. I gave them anything they needed—even drew in allies from other tribes!

My hands move on their own, ripping the flesh of my chest. Hot blood seeps, runs slowly down my body in eight thickening streams as I scream at the sky.

One moment of pure agony flashes in my brain when Longbow's hatchet cuts into my throat. My vision fades to black, but I still feel the lifeblood pour down my breast.

Chapter 50: Hawk
Chawathil Reborn

In rebuilding at Chawathil, our first task is to raise the rest of the logs for the wall. The smaller winches on sledges—the ones we built Highwater's walls with—will pull down any logs that are too burned to trust. The slaves drag newly cut trees to the site and dig the trench to set them in. Once the logs are in place, and with all the bodies working on the project, we have the perimeter and the wall up in slightly under fourteen suns.

Boomer sent half of the guards and slaves to Chawathil yesterday to clean up and clear away as much damage as they can so reconstruction can start right away when the rest of the workers arrive.

Those workers who remain cut cedars and start splitting planks. Normally they would be stacked for a year to dry, but structures are needed immediately and the wall planks will have to go up last. The residents can cut and split more and let them season for next year. For now, houses go up with green pole frames. The planks are cross-stacked, waiting to be used. They won't be fully seasoned, but they won't be completely green.

Wei shows us how to cut long grasses, dry them quickly, and bundle them for use as roofing. We aren't sure about the idea, but both Song assure us it is a technique that has been used in their home country for thousands of years. Terrible storms arrive in certain seasons, they say. Zizhan promises to stay and help with the thatching of the roofs while Wei goes to Xwelich.

Two builders who helped make the wall walks and covers for Highwater will stay behind at Chawathil to direct the construction of those. Since the protective walls aren't structural, they will be planked right away to provide protection in case of another attack. Everyone is watchful, aware of the missing force of Grasslanders.

Many hands make for quick work. One moon after starting repairs, the main body of workers leave for Chawathil.

***

It's another beautiful morning. Sunlight warms the meadows, lush and high with grasses and flowering plants and buzzing with the flying insects that pollinate them. The River and streams roar in freshet, slowly dropping, as most of the snow is off all but the highest mountains.

I lean on the front rail of the wall walk at Highwater, worrying some things over in my mind. It's time for the People to move down to Fishcamp. Fishcamp is, or was, exactly that: a long-term camp for the fishing seasons that run from late Spring to Fall. The salmon the People catch is needed for food for the whole year. It is eaten fresh, smoked, and air dried in Summer. It is our staple protein, a gift from the River. Our whole culture is based on it, but Fishcamp is not defensible, as far as I can see, and still some Grassland raiders remain unaccounted for. But all of the wind-drying racks, smokehouses, and other structures are gone, burned to the ground.

I think I need to consult with Fisheagle's older, wiser point of view. The Chief has been in constant contact with communities all around us, some many days', even weeks', travel from Highwater. The Grasslanders are now a regional problem. We need to find them or confirm that they have gone home, and if we can't, come up with a defense plan for Fishcamp and rebuild.

We promised trade goods for the Song when they return, and it is about time, according to Wei and Zizhan. We trapped and hunted over the Winter and have a good supply of furs, but we were not able to mine copper in the frozen months. We collected some before the snow flew and after the melt, before the Grasslanders came, but it is not a great amount. We have had more pressing issues.

Climbing down the ladder, I make my way to the Chief's house. Fisheagle welcomes me in and we sit at the large new table that Woodshaper made using the Song design, but a bit taller for us. He also provided eight four-legged stools to match the table, all made from the tall bigleaf maples that grow near the River. Properly dried, the wood is bright white and as hard as the white stones we see in the gravel at the River's edge. Many of the People collect them and place them in bowls of water for decoration. Some are almost as clear as the water.

Fisheagle looks at me. "What's worrying you? You're starting to look like me, with big creases between your eyes."

I can't help but grin and explain what is on my mind.

Fisheagle shakes his head. "Why are you worrying about those things? You don't have enough of your own things to worry about, that you have to worry about my things?" He chuckles. "Perhaps I should make a report to the People. They will have some of the same questions, especially when I tell them that we will only fish for fresh salmon this year."

"What!?" bursts from my mouth. I know enough about Fisheagle to hold my shocked questions until he finishes.

He smiles and nods. "Dried and smoked fish will come from several of the Alliance villages, so it is not a burden on any one. We have fresh, smoked, and dried meat coming in. You should build a cold storage place or two—somewhere to keep it all. We will pool our furs… In fact, we need to send ours to Rivergrass. They are collecting all of the Alliance trade goods. Li is excited about the sea otter furs. He says that Zahn will give us very good trade for those. Kiapelaneh has acquired rock coal from the Big Island and sulfur from several northern bands, who also have been mining copper since the snowmelt. Chen is smelting the copper from the rock and casting odd-looking rounds for trade, very unlike the shields we use. He says Zahn will be pleased. The last thing, I think, is that we have no word or sign of the missing raiders. Both you and I have had people out looking in all directions, and I exchange messages with villages at some distance. Perhaps our estimates of their numbers were wrong. Perhaps they fled back home after their defeat. We may never know until peace is reached with them." The Chief grins. "Anything else you worry about?"

I shake my head. "I should have known you were on top of all of it, and yes, you should let the People know what's happening. Now I can draft some workers for other projects that need doing. Not that we've had a shortage of willing hands for anything, with all the refugees and some slaves that we never had before."

Fisheagle looks up at my last comment. "How are the slaves being treated?"

"Pretty well, considering. I haven't seen or heard of anyone being cruel to them. Some of the youngsters taunt them a bit. Nothing serious yet."

The Chief nods. "I will put a stop to it. The Grasslander slaves were fooled and tempted into wrong actions. They will learn from the experience, and perhaps even win their freedom. Our People must know their leaders are compassionate, even to enemies.

"On another note, do you have your Chief's regalia yet? You will need it soon."

"I think my mother and sister are almost done. We have a blanket that belonged to my great-grandfather, who was Chief in Skawalook a long time ago. I barely remember him."

"Good! It has history. Put something of your own on it. It should remind you of the responsibility you bear for the good of the People."

We say our goodbyes. I need to do some thinking based on the new information. It seems there's always something I should worry about on my mind these days, but Fisheagle took a large weight off my shoulders. I didn't say it, but I have felt the obligation to help members of the community in times of need for some time. I have always pushed myself to take on duties. Our community gives more than they take. I will do what is asked of me.

Chapter 51: Hawk Alliance Expanding

True to his words to me, Fisheagle calls a meeting of everyone in Highwater, except those few on watch. He lays a hand on my arm in passing. "Wear your regalia to the meeting. You're a Chief now."

I nod and run home to dress for ceremony. As I enter my parents' house, my mother turns with her hands on her hips. "About time! You have your first ceremony as Chief and you're not even dressed yet! Stand *there*."

She points to a spot and I obey.

"Humph. The pants are fine for now, but I will start work on a new pair—all beaded, with some copper. Hold still while I put your robe on." She drapes it over my shoulders, then folds a beautifully woven blanket lengthwise and swathes it from one shoulder across my chest and pins it at my waist on the other side. "As is custom, you should award your blanket to whoever you feel most deserves it. Now your hat."

She steps back and looks me over. "You'll do. I'll be along shortly, if I can find your father…"

She turns away. Dismissed, I walk to the door, thinking about all the People have accomplished here.

We added onto the longhouse again, given our larger population. It is still being finished, but everyone fits inside. We are lacking some houses, but they too are in the works. If we gain more people, we are going to have to build another town, or expand beyond the walls. As I think about that, it appeals to me: a second wall, farther out. A town within a town. If the outer wall is breached, we can fall back, and the enemy will have to try to breach again with a lot fewer warriors for the second go. They might even be discouraged enough to go away.

I find myself grinning and realize that I stand at the door to the lodge and people are starting to notice. I put on my serious face, find a seat next to Midnight, and focus on Fisheagle, who stands to start the meeting. It is surprising to see him in full regalia for an information-sharing meeting of the People. Those are usually pretty informal—basically like family.

Come to think of it, why am I in ceremonial garb? And why do I see more tables and chairs than I recall from this morning?

Ts'aak of the Haida strides slowly from behind a curtain of blankets at the back of the lodge, wearing *his* full regalia, followed by ten more Haida, also in formal regalia, signaling an official visit. Something profound is about to happen. It is good to see that Ts'aak is a Chief now. For all his bluster, he has a good heart.

Fisheagle faces the newcomers. "Welcome, Chief Ts'aak! Your timing is excellent. Before you share the reason for your visit, please make yourselves comfortable. I will report to my people what has happened over the last few moons. You may find the information interesting as well, although you know some of it and may have heard more. I believe you hear many things…" He lets silence linger for a beat, with a little quirk at the corner of his lips as the Haida grin. "Then we will all be pleased to listen to your news."

Ts'aak extends his hand to the Chief, as do his followers. A young woman leads them to a space near the front.

Kiapelaneh of Rivergrass comes from the curtain next, followed by nine of his people, also in full regalia, his council of village chiefs. Behind his party comes another group led by Whalehunter, from the Kwakwaka'wakw, with his chiefs. Behind them is Stormrider of the Heiltsuk People and Tall-Raven from the Nuxalk, who have come almost as far as Ts'aak.

Fisheagle welcomes them all in the same warm, formal fashion as he did Ts'aak's delegation, with the same message—to wait for an announcement.

After a fragile moment of silence, Fisheagle opens his arms wide. His voice changes. "River People!" booms out of him.

The People answer with one voice. "People of the River!"

"We stopped a terrible threat to all of us in this region." He stops and Midnight screams her undulating cry of defiance. The People join in, shaking dust from the ceiling with the rolling thunder of it.

The reverberation stops, the dust settles, and a window of silence opens. Fisheagle breaks it.

"We accomplished this with the help and support of our friends and allies, Kiapelaneh and the Rivergrass People. Zizhan, Chen, Wei, and Li of the Song, an old and wise people from a land far to the west across the Great Water, have taught us many useful things and have many others they will share in trade. All of us here have engaged in that practice for most of our lives. When one has surplus, they exchange goods for what they need from others, so we have all benefited. Now I propose that we strengthen those ties further, through an Alliance. No one people to be subservient to any others: rather, we will support each other, as has always been our way within each of our People. Now we would extend that way of being beyond our traditional tribal lands. Nor will we lose our individual identities, for those come from the land and our ancestors."

That receives a resounding rumble in agreement.

Fisheagle continues. "The Song trader Zahn returns soon with more new ways of doing things, like the walls of this village, our arrowheads—of which a hundred can be produced in a day—and the winches that allow us to move great tree trunks with ease and operate the rising bridge you all walked in over. They have knowledge of making metal tools that are stronger and easier to use than those we have now. The Song safely travel the Great Water in canoes that make ours look like children's toys."

He stops at a murmur of excitement and some disbelief from a few of the guests from the Big Island who haven't met the Song yet. The delegations mumble among themselves, and the Chief lets them. When the noise dies down, he resumes.

"So long as they are willing to share knowledge for copper and hides, I will trade with them. They agreed to bring tools this time, which will give us a chance to try the results of their knowledge. If they are as good as I think they will be, we will gain knowledge from their design. But we also desire the understanding of how their tools are made and how they work. If the materials are much better than what we have—and so far, they have been—we want to know how to make those materials ourselves."

Nodding heads mark the point made. They are all shrewd traders with wide networks, reaching even into the plains to the east, and see the wisdom in Fisheagle's words.

"I asked you here to share our thoughts with you. If we all have the same goals in our negotiations, we negotiate in strength and they will meet our terms. If they can acquire the goods they seek for easier terms, they will. That is simply good trading. If we speak with one voice, then the terms will be more favorable. This works well for them, too. They will gain better products as we develop better skills and goods. Perhaps we will advance, together, beyond what any of our People could have done alone."

I feel the excitement in the room as guests and locals alike digest his words and begin to share his vision.

Fisheagle scans the delegations, pausing briefly at each. It's impressive. Never have I seen the Chief so alive and passionate, so powerful. This is a seed planted, but it will need time to grow. He has pushed us all in the direction of his vision for our future, and events will unfold as they will. In time, I feel we can nudge a bit as needed.

He raises both hands, open palms toward them all, then sits. It is the signal for the feast to begin.

Chapter 52: Narrator
The Best of Worlds

The future was in motion. It swirled from the east, the west, north, and south. A Song ship, a vibrant coastal culture eager for new opportunities, a stagnant inland culture driven by greed, and a southern culture ready for change: all unknowingly waited for something.

As present became past, bringing the future closer, events unfolded, following the path of the ship from the east. Precisely as in battle, some die that others can live.

In the best of worlds, some deaths save the lives of many others.

Chapter 53: Zahn
Return

I slow my ship to a crawl and guide it as close to the rocky cliff as I dare. Looking over the side, I see jagged fingers of stone ready to rip our keel off, but deep water is there, I know, for this is our third visit to the Haida.

I finally find the deep hollow next to shore where I have anchored before. It allows for easy access to the land and I can relax a bit now. I put the rudders over and drift the ship gently in, parallel to the landing. We have a plank long enough to reach the rocks on the shore. The crew pushes it out, and two sailors run across with ropes to secure us close, but not too close yet, to the rocky shore. The crew casts woven bamboo mats attached to ropes at one end over the side to take the shock of the rocks if waves throw the ship against them. Then the sailors on shore pull the ship up tighter, leaving room for the rise and fall of the tides.

I stride down the plank and greet Chief Ts'aak. We exchange pleasantries, and with the formalities out of the way, Ts'aak opens negotiations.

"If you come with me, we have our goods in the warehouse. I look forward to seeing what you have brought." He smiles...quite genuinely, I think.

The goods please me: furs, well cured, and including many of the coveted golden sea otters that live nowhere else in the world but along this coast; a goodly number of copper ingots; and more Haida artwork that I tried in the Shanghai markets on the previous voyage. The works proved very popular in the Song capital. Their esthetic is similar to ours, but taken in some very interesting new directions.

Ts'aak waits, silent, for the first offer.

"I have a variety of hard, long-lasting tools, some beautiful fabrics..."

Ts'aak smiles. "Your tools, depending on what they do, interest me. Even more interesting to me is an advisor, such as you left with the southern tribes—preferably one who can teach us how to make the hard metal for tools, and the tools themselves."

I stop still, shocked at his forthrightness and sagacity. My face burns. Usually I have a firm grip on my reactions, but he surprised me. No longer smiling, I ask, "Do you plan to ruin my trade, then?"

Ts'aak laughs. "Of course not. As I said, your tools are interesting, but tools break, and it is many moons before you return. If we become dependent on your tools, which will change the way we work, and then they don't work anymore, we are left in an uncomfortable position. Surely you see that."

"Very well. Your copper, as shown, for the use of one of my men for the time between now and my next voyage."

He's thrown me off balance. These people are astute traders, but this is an even harder bargain than I am used to from them.

I could spare one of my shipwrights who can teach them what they want, but I hate to do so. These savages now are more astute than I gave them credit for, and it will impact my profit. I consider alternatives with instincts honed in the cutthroat markets of Shanghai, Heian-kyō, and Kaesong. I calculate as quickly as I can, not wanting to be seen as hesitant or unwilling.

I will be able to pick up the four shipwrights I left farther south. They will have had enough of these primitives. So what if they learn to make iron and work it? Many, many other things that I can offer will fill my hold on future voyages. I determine to be better prepared next time. I bow acceptance.

Ts'aak also bows his agreement to the deal. "Now, let's see these tools of yours."

I signal my sailors to bring ashore samples of iron augers, hatchets, axes, pry bars, and saws of various sizes, from one-handed to long two-man saws for planking. I display hammers and kegs of metal nails of various sizes. One of my sailors demonstrates their use in joining two pieces of wood.

Ts'aak considers, then haggles with me for a time. The nails don't impress him, but the other tools do. Finally he offers their furs for a selection of tools. We agree on the quantities of each and move on.

Ts'aak suggests, "We do have some artwork we would trade for your fabrics, if they are acceptable…"

I feel better—this is easy trade. "Let's inspect the goods and reach agreement then."

Ts'aak smiles and bows his own concurrence.

The Haida take all of the fabric I have to trade in return for their extraordinary artwork, which reflects similarities to antique Song designs. That made them very popular, and profitable, in the Empire on the previous voyages, and the Haida seem to feel a kindred artistic sense in the Song fabrics.

I left one of my shipwrights, an excellent worker with a talent for solving problems and knowledge of both wood and metal. His name is Dù, which is tattooed on his right forearm: 杜. I don't see him here.

Chapter 54: Narrator
Plague

Two weeks later, the disease struck. Those affected started with a mild illness: fever, headache, and body pain. Then it spread across the skin as little bubbles that burgeoned and grew.

People began to die by the tens, then hundreds.

The blisters on those who survived scabbed over and were endured for the rest of their lives as many small dark hollows on the victims' skin.

In the end, two-thirds of the Haida died. Some were blinded in one or both eyes.

Chapter 55: Zahn
Return on Investment

I sail my ship south along the coast, eager to arrive at the village where I have invested four of my shipwrights to create a market for my remaining cargo. Tools are heavy, so I hope to unload the lot at Rivergrass. I am eager to see if the southerners have collected a good quantity of sea otter pelts and copper refined with smelters built by my shipwrights. I also want to see the quality of the greenstone they spoke of. If it *is* a new variety of jade, my fortune is made.

Eagerness makes me pass by a couple of communities I have traded with before on the way down the coast. I can always stop in on my next voyage. They do have some nice artwork.

It has been a good journey, if long. We finally come around a forested and rocky headland and the Rivergrass delta opens before me. My ship's name is *Hǎishàng Qíshǒu* [Sea Rider], and I direct the crew toward the new wharf that Chen and Li designed and built at my instruction. It stretches across the tidal flat to a deeper hole where the ship can tie up. I see the sailors have also made wheeled carts, now lined up on the pier to move the heavy tools down the boardwalk to the shore.

I have, in fact, brought civilization to these people. It gives me a sense of pride I did not expect. I was but one of many traders who might have chosen to follow the current. It so happened that I *was* the first and discovered new markets. I find myself looking forward to seeing the other changes my shipwrights have wrought among these people, and the trade goods, of course. Copper is rising in price at home, and the furs always do well when I bring them back to Shanghai.

Other captains took note of my last profitable voyage. The wharf at home is a spy-ridden place, and the traders are the most cunning in the known world. My crew knows to be silent, on pain of flogging…or worse. Still, every cargo I deliver could be the last as the sole trader in this new market. That is one reason why I left the advisors—to establish goodwill for future voyages. So long as I have first rights, I will profit greatly. My trader sense tells me great potential exists here. I can smell advantage!

As soon as we are tied to the pier, I order the tools brought up and loaded into the carts. I see the natives, and Li and Chen, on the shore. I hope Wei and Zizhan will bring the second tribe along soon. This being my first Spring voyage, I can possibly make two more voyages before the winter weather confines us to local Empire trade, which is not nearly as profitable.

I was able to purchase a compass with part of the proceeds from the last voyage. It allows me to cut straight across the Sea to home instead of following the route way up north, around the Big Island, then down the coast, battling violent currents and cold boils of deeps in turmoil on the last long reach to the open ocean. Coming here, I travel with the currents, and during my first three voyages, I had to sail back against those same currents. It was a long, slow voyage, but without the compass, we might have ended up anywhere if I simply pointed the ship across the Sea. Once out of sight of land I have the stars, until a storm comes, or if the skies are even overcast. Then I had nothing to guide us…until now. With the compass, we can navigate straight home to Shanghai, a happy conclusion to a surely profitable voyage.

Stepping onto the plank, I realize that the coastal village they call Rivergrass now has a log palisade around it, a drawbridge over a ditch, and a covered walk at the top. Turning to the south, I see a line of three huge cargo canoes headed from upriver to the wharf all loaded, sitting deep in the water.

I maintain my outward composure despite a powerful inner surge of glee. I will return with the *Hǎishàng Qíshǒu's* holds full, by the look of things. Hurrying, but trying to act casually, I walk down the plank to the wharf, moving toward the dock where the canoes are pulling in and tying up in a row.

Chen and Li are walking out from the Rivergrass beach to meet me. I see Kiapelaneh waiting to greet me as well. Zizhan and Wei climb out of the lead cargo canoe, followed by the older Chief and a native man and woman. Dozens of other people sit in the canoes. I have a twinge of uneasiness, but I still manage to beam delightedly at the three from upriver. Zizhan is here to translate for me.

"My good friends! Well met. I brought the tools we discussed. I hope my advisors have been worth their keep?"

The younger Chief speaks. "Indeed, wise Zahn. You are most welcome back, and your people have been of inestimable value to us. We would have been in great difficulty if they had not been here to share your ways of thinking and doing. That said, we have much to compensate you and to trade for tools."

He smiles widely at me, and I suddenly have a memory of Ts'aak driving a very hard bargain not so long ago.

"'Great difficulty?' Why? What has happened?"

"We will tell you the story tonight at a feast. It is too long of a tale to tell before we discuss our business. It would be sleep time before we conclude our trade!"

I nod my head. "A mighty tale, then. Very well, to business."

I show them my goods, plus tongs to handle hot metal and other tools to remove crucibles of molten metal from the ovens. The demonstration of the nails is greeted much more favorably here, and it is good the Haida didn't want any. The natives seem pleased. I also have about fifty small kegs of niter toward our common interest in copper.

Kiapelaneh shares that they found a local source of the rock coal and plenty of sulfur. Then we walk down the wharf to the canoes from Highwater. Protective tarps have been untied and now are pulled away to show their goods. The first canoe holds furs from land mammals: fox, wolf, marten, freshwater otter, lynx, beaver, a few cougar and bear, and also some deer and moose hides, expertly tanned with the hair on. The second canoe holds more of the same.

The third is full of copper, in Song-style ingots, and also a few ingots of a metal with a much richer color, which I know instantly are gold. Carts begin to arrive from the village holding sea mammal furs: sea otter, seal, and sea lion, and more ingots of copper.

This is astounding. For a moment, I have no words. Obviously, these people can supply as much as I can carry home, and the profits will be beyond my previous imagination. *The sea otter pelts alone will pay for this voyage!*

I look at the native leaders and I see in their eyes that they know the value of their goods. My own men, whom I left here, are looking at me with suspicious doubt and concern.

Then the River People unveil a pile of green rocks, some large, some small. Jade, and unlike any jade I have ever seen.

My legs go weak, so I sit down on the edge of the wharf and hold my head in my hands. *I have to think.* If I bring this load back, every trader on the coast of the Song Dynasty will follow me wherever I go for the rest of my life to find out where I have procured this cargo. The other side of the coin is that if I don't trade fairly with these people, they will never trade with me again. I see it in their eyes. *They know*!

I cast a glance at Wei, Li, Chen, and Zizhan. All four stare intensely at me with cold, hard eyes, awaiting my response. I believe they send me a silent message as well. I see they allude to a story of deadly import here. I need to know more before I do anything, or I may lose it all.

***

I stand and face them. "I think I must hear this tale. You have surpassed my highest hopes for this voyage. Shall we go to your lodge and let me hear the account? We can talk about trade later."

My own men are surprised. I can't really read the natives, except they look more at ease, as if relieved. I order all of my men, except for three, to stand watch on the ship and the tools, to come to the lodge with me. Whatever this is, I know in my gut it is deadly important to both the natives and my own men who have been here.

Entering the lodge, we see tables loaded with food. They are proper tables, although a bit taller than usual, with benches for everyone to sit on. The building is packed. Wei leads me to a prime seat beside the Chief, Fisheagle, and introduces Midnight and Hawk on the other side, whom I recognize from my last voyage.

An older woman strides confidently to the front of the crowd and is announced as Huckleberry, The Keeper of Stories from Highwater. Silence reigns in the hall. Zizhan has scooched forward so he can translate for me.

Huckleberry begins the tale of Hawk and Midnight, of the evil Shaman and his greed. She recalls the preparations for war and honors the Song advisors. She speaks of the battles, the rescues, and the dead, then of the reconstruction of the villages destroyed. She tells of an Alliance forged and growing, honoring Fisheagle for his wisdom in that. She relates a vision of people across the vast expanse of this land, to the north, south, and east, joining together to build something greater than villages in the wilderness: an Alliance!

A new commitment guided by a Council of Chiefs based on their reverence for the land, the spirits of nature, and their ancestors for the good of all the peoples who live on this vast land. Trade will benefit all parties. Governance will benefit all the People. The land, its spirits, and its People are the central concern of this new Alliance, and those who would help it are a welcome part of it. Those who oppose it are doomed, for all of the forces of the natural world and the spirit world will fight with the People when that day comes. The Alliance will be their voice and mighty arm against their enemies, and none of those will survive the experience. The Alliance's People will live in peace.

When she finishes, a moment of reverent quiet holds, then someone begins an undulating scream of defiance. It builds to almost deafening force, then fades like a spent wave returning to the Sea.

I sit still as stone, my mind racing at the implications. This is an Empire being born, and I am here to witness it.

Zizhan leans forward again, speaking in our tongue. "Chen, Li, Wei, and I will not be returning with you. We have found a place of honor here, where we can be more than we ever believed possible. We thank you for that, but know our allegiance has changed. Help these People, help us, and your rewards will outstrip your imagination. You will always be first—for the best items at the best price. There is much more to this place and its people than first meets the eye, and we don't even know yet how big it is."

It's astounding. Somehow, my simple trading voyages have changed the world for these people, and they know what to do with it. Astute traders indeed! Alliance?! All I have seen in all my travels is Empire and collections of villages. I know I need time to process what I have heard, to understand where to go with this and what to do next. The world has changed. *What to do? What to do?* swirls in my mind, but no question arises whether these people can accomplish forging their Empire, or Alliance, as they call it.

My profit from what the People brought will buy ships, as well as goods, but I sense also their need for knowledge above all. I can deliver that. Perhaps even, in time, I can help them reach the level of technology and science my own people have achieved. These minds will take that and go farther—perhaps even beyond my own culture.

One day, I may even be taking knowledge in the opposite direction, benefiting my people as much as theirs.

Chapter 56: Narrator
One Canoe

One canoe came from the north. One man paddled alone, untouched by death. He glided in silence up to the wharf at Rivergrass.

He slung a loop over a piling and placed a foot on it, still, hunched as a dark lump, not touching the shore or even the wharf.

Zahn's ship still waited at the end, and two of Zahn's men stood watch. One of the guards, Chan-Su, walked down the ramp and approached the canoe.

The man waved him away, pointing at the longhouse.

He spoke in a Song dialect. "Bring Kiapelaneh and Zahn now. This is important."

Startled, Chan-Su looked back at Zahn's ship, ran to the plank, and shouted to the other guard, "I must go to the Captain!"

His partner waved and Chan-Su sprinted away. Once inside the lodge, he went straight to Zahn and whispered a quick report.

Chapter 57: Zahn
Dù and Death

I stand and turn to Wei, who is closest. "A man in a Haida canoe has just arrived. He wears a hood over his face and he won't leave his canoe. He speaks the language of the Empire and asks for Kiapelaneh and myself." I nod to Fisheagle, who hurries over.

Wei goes first to Hawk and Midnight. Fisheagle swivels around to listen as Wei quietly explains the situation. His trade tongue is quite good now.

The hall is silent. Everyone watches curiously, aware that something significant is happening. Fisheagle stands and waves urgently to Kiapelaneh, who rises and joins them. They speak for a moment, then stride urgently out toward the wharf, Wei, myself, and others following. The buzz rising among those who remain in the hall fades behind us.

The Rivergrass Chief arrives at the dock first. He approaches the man in the canoe, but the man waves him back. He sees the rest of us coming.

"Keep them away!"

Then he tells us all what has happened at the Haida village, speaking in the trade tongue. He describes an illness starting as a mild affliction, like the stomach sickness that comes around to some every year. But this progresses.

He speaks of hundreds of bodies, and the scarring and crippling aftereffects on the survivors.

"Keep back! Help us, please. Our battle with the sickness has taken all our energy and resources. Spread the word that disease is alive in our villages. Keep back! It is upon me, even though I am immune."

I listen to the story with growing horror, grab Kiapelaneh by the arm, and summon Wei.

"I know what this is."

Wei translates what I say, and all eyes are on me.

"We call it the 'small-pocks' because it leaves small round scars in the skin of the survivors. Do you not have this here?"

All of the natives sign No.

I groan and my stomach cramps, leaving me short of breath. This place has never been exposed to the disease. It kills untold numbers every year, especially in remote parts of the Empire where people are less likely to have been given the vaccine.

I collapse into a sitting position on the wharf.

I don't know how, but I brought it. The timing is perfect.

My swirling mind remembers bits of details: The disease takes about twelve days to show. Within a moon, many are dead, more scarred and crippled.

It has clearly flourished here in an untouched population. In the Empire, many have had the disease or have been immunized.

I motion to Wei. "Bring this man food and drink, but do not touch him. He may still have the disease about him."

Wei runs off to the longhouse.

"We will help you, and the Haida people, but carefully so we don't spread the disease."

Wei returns with several others bearing blankets and preserved food and places the supplies on the edge of the wharf within the man's easy reach. With my eyes fixed on the ground, I speak to those who followed us from the lodge.

"We have this disease where we come from—it is in all the lands we trade with. It kills many and cripples more. Somehow it must have arrived with us. None of my people were sick, so I have no idea how it traveled…"

Understanding bursts in my mind with a sudden memory: a scrawny, bedraggled vendor who approached me as I prepared to depart from the main island of the Heian people, northeast of Shanghai, on the way here. He seemed almost desperate to sell a few bolts of silk very cheap. I naturally pounced on the deal, thinking the seller was in financial difficulty. Perhaps the bolts were even stolen, but provenance is no matter to me.

I face the onlookers, "The disease shows within twelve days of exposure, so none of my people could have carried it. It had to have been in the Heian silk I traded to the Haida, dormant." Horror overwhelms me. "When they unrolled the cloth…" I choke on emotions and can't go on.

I know Wei understands. I vaguely hear his voice, translating my points and explaining that the disease can't be on any of the other trade goods. *No more. Please, no more.*

Tears overflow as I clasp my midsection and rock back and forth, sick with responsibility. I don't know who hears my words or understands.

"We placed the bolts directly into a dry compartment especially made for goods that can be damaged by moisture. Even if the ship sank, it would be some time before the Sea could penetrate. When the bolts were removed from dry storage, they were presented to the Haida for inspection. They unrolled it, and we never touched it again. The dormant cysts must have been inside the rolls. The Haida traded for all of the cloth we picked up on that island."

I look up, finally. "The Haida survivors must be isolated, or the disease will spread like fire in a summer-dry forest. We know no cure once the sickness takes hold, but… Our healers know how to make people untouchable by the disease. It is a simple thing."

A darkness clouds my soul. "A simple thing," I mutter. "A simple thing…"

Fisheagle is speaking. "…bring one or more of these medicine men … teach us how to protect ourselves…"

Now Wei: "With what trade goods … return with several … safely make the medicine. … huge project to stop it. Every person has to be treated, and every child who is born…"

Sooner or later the People will begin to have more contact with the outside world. More ships mean more chances for this and other diseases of body and spirit to be carried here.

Abruptly I rise and force myself to stand in respect and honor of the dead. I look around at all the People and my shipwrights. "I am responsible for this. I will do everything I can think of to help."

Kiapelaneh nods solemnly. "It appears the source of our good fortune can also be a source of great trouble. It seems somehow fitting, a balance… I think I must travel with Zahn, our fearless and honest trader."

A communal gasp escapes from the crowd of Rivergrass People, many of whom have come out to the wharf to see what is happening.

Kiapelaneh smiles. "Do not fear, for I leave you in good hands. I must be the eyes of the People to see what this other world looks like and discover, as I can, what it has to offer…and what other dangers may come to us. I will be the first of our People to try this new medicine. Then I can know it is safe. I will take a few other witnesses with me, if that is acceptable to our trader Captain?"

My mind has slipped back into itself and I only vaguely hear the translation, but I nod agreement. My gut is knotted and my mouth and tongue are dry and gummy. I have never felt heartsick before, but that term well describes my feelings now. I, my beloved *Hǎishàng Qíshǒu,* and my crew have effectively wiped out at least one village of gentle people: artists and craftspeople; mothers, fathers, and children.

I thought myself a hard, strong man until this day. I have fought raiders and pirates, and have always negotiated for maximum return…unless it made sense to suck in the client first, and then rape his wallet.

This is different.

This has the potential to annihilate an entire civilization if it runs loose in this land where it has never been.

They have no resistance to it. It will kill and kill and kill, and maim the few who do survive.

I have brought it.

My spirit is lost in the vast horror of my responsibility. I barely notice when Chen and Li support and guide me into the ship, to my cabin, where they wrap a blanket around me and lay me down in my bunk.

My Chief Officer of the Boat, WanLi, brings me a bottle of rice wine and stays with me. I battle the horror with the wine, which helps me face the demons who bring me images of villages strewn with corpses and the feeble twitches of the dying.

The bottle is empty.

***

My Captain slurs, "WanLi! More wine!"

I recognize shock when I see it and obediently bring another bottle. I also know he is a kind and civilized man beneath the hard trader persona he adopts for business.

He has never mistreated a crewman who made an honest mistake. Having served on many ships as I learned my trade, I know Zahn is an exceptional Captain and man.

I hope his despair will pass soon.

Chapter 58: Kiapelaneh
For Good or Evil

Back at the lodge, I announce my intention to travel with Zahn on his return voyage. "Our world is changing because of this other culture across the Great Water. I now know with certainty that Zahn is an honest and good man. I trust him to return me to you on his voyage back. I will do my job as Chief and represent our People to theirs. I hope to speak to their leaders and gain a sense of who they are.

"I will also see what their culture has brought them, for good and for evil. We have now learned a lesson on the perils of ignorance. Entire Haida villages—thankfully, not all—were effectively wiped out. We must know more about what we are dealing with. We must understand when to say 'no' to what seem like gifts, or even fair trade. This disaster was an accident, but perhaps some in their society would do this on purpose. Think of the Grassland Shaman, who would have enslaved us all and taken our ancestral lands. Men of that type live there as well as here, and if they are lesser evils, they are evil nonetheless. We must have a sense of the threat. Zahn has already said other ships will follow him when they see what he has brought home from his visit here."

My words spark a hum of discussion and a full gamut of emotions reflects from the faces of the People. Now they understand the possible impact of contact with this new world beyond the Great Sea.

Fisheagle walks over to speak with me. We find a table in the back to talk for some time. No one bothers us.

Chapter 59: Dù
Dù Departs

The People bring supplies: blankets, food, and other things, as much as the canoe will hold safely, and ask me what else they can do for me or the Haida people.

"Spread the word to all of the villages and communities to stay away. Those of us left will survive, but we do not want this to happen to anyone else. We will run off any traders who come. If you have the cure, come to us, but not before."

Someone asks for my name, for the histories.

I think for a moment. "I am not the man I used to be. My name is Darkwater from this day forward, and this has become my history."

I let the tether to the dock slip and draw it back to my canoe. I, Dù, now Darkwater, a lone man in one canoe, push my oar against the wharf, spin the canoe, and paddle north.

David Oliver-Godric

Chapter 60: Midnight Chá and Farewell

I sense Zahn is better by morning when he arrives at the longhouse. He joins us for breakfast, bringing a box with him that he gives to a Song cook.

Hawk, myself, Fisheagle, Kiapelaneh, and the Song advisors make room at the Chief's table. It is quiet, even somber in the ordinarily noisy longhouse. A short time later, one of the cooks brings an enameled tray with a steaming pot with a handle and spout, an open pot containing a thick liquid that looks like honey, and eight delicate cups, all carved from a pale greenstone and ornately decorated. I admire the cups, their raised flowers, trees, and birds, and wonder how they shape and polish the stone so intricately. Zahn pours liquid from the spout into each of the cups and hands them around the table.

"This is chá," Chen translates and smiles. "I asked Zahn to bring back a good supply on his next voyage. I have missed it. Your willow bark tea is not the same, though it does ease the aches of labor. You may find chá as refreshing as we do. The pot contains honey. You may wish to add a little sweetener, but try it plain first. Bring the pot to the cup, then pull out the stick from the honey and let the honey drizzle into the tea."

I sip carefully as it is still steaming hot. The chá is bitterly delicious, a welcome restorative in the fresh morning air. The tangy warmth of it is pleasant as well. After a couple of sips, most everyone tries a little honey in it.

I taste love. The bitterness, blended with honey sweetness and the warmth of the water, embodies the experience of life! My eyelids sag to slits of contentment and I smile peacefully. Then a gentle rush of energy nudges my eyes fully open. I grin.

Chen smiles back. "It is a stimulant as well."

I raise my head from the cup long enough to say, "Tell Zahn to double the order." Then I go back to sipping, holding the warm cup with both hands. Hawk laughs. Chen translates everyone's comments for Zahn, who summons a faint smile for the first time.

"Be aware, my friends, that chá does not grow in your climate. It likes the heat of southern lands. I will endeavor to keep you supplied, but it is one of the most valuable and sought-after trade goods in the world. However, with your new jade, you can afford it. You might even be able to grow some in areas farther south. It likes a lot of heat and moisture, but not too wet."

News that it will be a trade good inspires a cheer from all those in earshot and spreads as the atmosphere of confidence at the front table inspires our People to optimism despite the horror of the night before. Conversation perks up throughout the hall.

Chapter 61: Zahn
A Change of Plans

Finally composed and able to think rationally again, I start to plan. I need to make the round trip as quickly as possible to start the inoculations and bring physicians to begin training the local healers in our medical knowledge. I also want to see how well the new jade is received by Song artisans. I will almost certainly need to present some bits to officials as bribes to resolve any "problems" in a speedy manner, but that will also help to establish a market. If someone has something new and rare, many others will desire it.

I used to know an ironsmith who might be interested in bringing his industry to the new land, and he may, in turn, be able to connect me with senior iron miners who can find and process the ore. Those three things—medicine, mining, and ironworking—will be the focus on this trip. Personally, I know nothing about iron mining.

So, recruit miners and physicians, introduce the new jade to the market, and make the Empire known to the natives who accompany me. That is enough for a quick turnaround trip.

My plans in place, I return my attention to chá and my companions. I note Midnight is on her second, possibly third, cup of chá.

I gesture to Chen to translate. "I want to leave as soon as possible. It's a long journey, and I want to unload and reload as fast as I can to return with the things we need to begin to stop this disease, and truly start your metal industry. It should leave me time to make at least one more trip before Winter. If other traders arrive with tools, feel free to trade whatever you have for them…but not the jade. That trade will be just between us. Agreed?"

The chiefs nod and I continue. "It will be years, at least, before we can locate iron ore, mine it, set up facilities to convert the ore into metal, and then teach your people how to work it. That's why I want to start as soon as we can. The tools I brought are steel, which is cunningly made from iron. It is tougher than plain iron, not as likely to break. If it gets wet, like iron, water will eat at it over time, so dry the tools when they get wet. I will bring back more steel tools as well. If you end up with more than you need, trade them to other tribes. It will expand your influence, and your circle of friends. Make sure you isolate the Grasslanders from the tool trade. That will be your advantage, and perhaps a bit of punishment!"

I flash a sly grin, returned by the chiefs when they hear the translation.

Midnight looks up. "Don't forget to leave room for chá!"

I can't help but grin as I take my last sip of chá, then rise and stroll across the sandy beach to the wharf and *Hǎishàng Qíshǒu* to supervise the unloading and loading. I find my crew working efficiently as always.

I only hire experienced hands, and any who don't work with my veterans are left behind, sometimes in strange places. It is an added incentive that none of my crew has missed. I haven't had to do that for some years now, but my Second makes sure the stories are told dramatically belowdecks. Ah, the tale of Kang, the onetime horseman from the northern steppes. He was hard as stone in a fight, but as venomous as a cave spider on the crew deck. He liked to cheat at games of chance, then beat the man who caught him at it. I left him in the hottest jungle I could find in the southern sea. He didn't speak the language. Occasionally, when I hear the story being told, I wonder how that worked out for him.

Smiling, I march onboard, take my place on the raised aft deck, and survey my domain. I love the *Hǎishàng Qíshǒu*. She has brought me though gales, squalls, and war zones—even the odd pirate attack. She is fast and very maneuverable for a merchant ship, but sturdy and carries heavy loads well. She is my first home, and my partner. I have never married, mainly because of the time I spend at sea. I have a modest house I visit two or three times a year, but it is more an investment and occasional convenience than home. I bought in a very desirable part of the city and hired a reliable couple to maintain it. They live in a comfortable cottage behind and keep the house ready at all times. None of us know when I might arrive.

Sometimes, during the long watches at sea, I think about retiring to land somewhere. *It may finally be that this market will bring the wealth I need to settle in a real home, perhaps even start a family.*

By noon, all of the cargo is unloaded. Content, I tell the crew to go to the longhouse and find something to eat. Looking around, I realize no one here is going to steal or damage anything and decide to join them. I have never before left my ship unguarded in a port, but here, no one will touch it. I marvel at the thought. Out of the many, many places I have traveled, this one breaks all the rules. Content with my decisions, I go for lunch.

Kiapelaneh asks me what I want for provisions on the voyage home and I tell the Chief what I already have onboard. Kiapelaneh makes some suggestions from the supplies he has on hand that he thinks will last the trip. I agree to most of it, but ask for some game meat packed in salt. Their deer meat is quite delicious and we have casks on board that are empty and will do. The Chief agrees and assigns four of his people to the task.

Loading and securing the load takes the rest of the afternoon. As dusk rolls in, I think about navigating the channels at night with all the tide rips and other anomalies populating these waters, and conclude we can wait for morning. I tell the crew they have done a good, professional job of work this day and give them one last night off: departure at dawn. Following a cheer from all hands, they troop to the longhouse and supper.

The morning farewells are brief. Kiapelaneh, with three of his men and two women, come aboard carrying large trapping packs. Zizhan arrives with a pack and offers to accompany the six guests aboard as translator for the journey, get them settled belowdecks, and explain the routine and rules of the boat underway. He will also translate and help them understand what they see. I know that he has an eye to starting a family with one of the local women, so I thankfully agree, and then fall into my habitual departure process.

The whole population of the village and all the Rivergrass guests pack the wharf to see us off. They are singing a song. Zizhan tells me it is a celebration of my voyage to them, sorrow at our leaving, and finally, a promise of welcome home again when we return.

"They might live in separate villages and territories, but they are truly beginning to act like one People, Zizhan. I guess I really should try to learn their language."

Zizhan nods. "You have some time on the voyage, and I will help you. The trade tongue is what you need to learn. It's understood everywhere. These people have a different language for almost every community. It's like they all came from different places, but the trade tongue unites them."

Chapter 62: Zahn
Traveling the Seas

The channel south winds around islands and random rocks that poke up in the middle of what look like clear stretches of water from a distance. Tide rips and whirlpools, some large enough to suck my ship down, suddenly appear, then disappear.

Hǎishàng Qíshǒu passes by a myriad of tiny islands and coves, plates of unbroken rock that go on for great stretches, and boils of upwelling water from untold deeps. The cliffs rise as a wall on the southern side of the channel. I have seen these phenomena before, but never so packed together in such a wide channel. I will forever recall the last long run.

Powerful swirls try to spin the ship, first one way, then the other. The helmsmen on the rudders are white-knuckled and ashen-faced, fighting immense forces. The soaring stone cliffs loom above, seeming to wait for us to lose control.

This battle lasts for most of the day, and then we are finally in normal water as the channel opens out. I record all of the individual dangers in my log and chart. The trip down from the north is complex, with hundreds of rocks barely above the surface, or lurking slightly under it, and many narrow channels that have to be taken at the right time on the tide. But the enormous power we experienced in this channel, and its approaches, is nothing I have ever seen before.

At the channel's end, we still have to cross the bar to open water. On previous trips, I retraced my route from the north, past the northern end of the Big Island, then headed south. I think the route north might be longer, but safer. We could manage the southern route in a pinch, but I'm sure my ruddermen would really rather not.

My goods will fetch the best price in the Empire, especially in the capitol. These are premium goods in quantities never seen before. I must plan my route to maximize future trade. Perhaps I should drop in to some secondary markets on the way. Give them a taste of what I can deliver…

Chapter 63: Midnight Gifts of the Empire

High Summer and a bright, warm morning bathes me in sunlight at Rivergrass when Zahn returns, and he doesn't come alone. Two other ships, similar but larger, follow behind. The wharf is long enough to dock them all, two to one side and the last on the other. Kiapelaneh and his entourage disembark first from the lead ship. Behind them are four older Song men in gorgeous shimmering silk robes, embroidered with birds, insects, and symbols that evoke clouds and faces. A few women elbow their partners or their friends. Many of our young women are almost drooling. I see one who actually does, wiping it away with her hand and staring some more. I watch her closely and follow them to the lodge.

Nosey and I arrived by canoe just today. It had been a while since I was at Rivergrass, and I wanted to hear any news that hadn't made it upriver yet. To be honest, I'm becoming anxious about Zahn and his promises. They may be wonderful things, as he suggested, but we've seen that good things often bring their own problems. We will have to solve those issues if we can. Nosey chitters agreement, so it seems.

Distracted by my wonderings, I missed some of Zahn's sailors starting to unload large wooden chests, which are also highly decorated and finished. I edge closer for a good look. The workmanship is beyond anything I've seen, even from our greatest carvers. The sailors carry them straight to the longhouse. Some of our native woodworkers swarm around the sailors carrying them in. I have never seen finishes like these. The base color is black, but it has the appearance of depth, like the night sky filled with the tiniest of sparkles, stars on a moonless night shining boldly in the void. The wood beneath is perfectly joined; no seams show through the coating. It is as if they were carved from a single block.

Seven middle-aged Song men with short stout bodies and massive arms and legs—compared to the lithe seamen—disembark next. Judging by the worn leather garb they wear and the tools they carry, I assume these are miners, whose task it will be to find iron deposits and plan mining operations. They carry their own equipment and personal goods.

I follow them to the longhouse, curious to see their reactions. During Zahn's absence, the Rivergrass longhouse expanded to more than double its previous size. It is quite an impressive structure now, with stunning story poles at all the corners and at the intermediate supports. I poke my head in for a quick look and see that some of the interior poles are carved and painted as well, telling stories of recent events. As I turn to leave, the door pole to the left of the entrance catches my eye and I stop before one that depicts Fisheagle, Hawk, and myself. I have never been honored in this way and it feels a bit…uncomfortable. *I wonder if Hawk will notice.* Shrugging, I walk on to see what other surprises await.

Many new houses have been erected in anticipation of an influx of people to this main trading post for the new Alliance, from both sides of the Great Water. The expansion is timely given that three ships are disgorging people and cargo. The goods are put in a second, much plainer structure, a storage building with a raised wooden floor to keep the tools and other items dry, as Zahn suggested before he left.

I want to see everything, so I circulate, peek at what is being unpacked, and ask questions where the goods are not immediately familiar. I drift back inside just as several wooden casks are delivered to the cooking area. Chen tells me they are probably sauces to add flavor to food. Outside I saw other casks that I learned hold herb and vegetable seeds that are familiar to the Song. Many large thin steel bowls with handles, which Li explains are for cooking, hang along wooden stands with metal hooks, apparently set up while I was outside. Bundles of mysterious metal and wooden tools also hang from racks or sit in clay pots, waiting for use.

More casks continue to be carried straight to the cooking area, along with many boxes that the bearers proceed to open. They unpack dozens of chá pots and cups, and honey pots with little wooden tools for getting the honey into the cup. Crocks of honey and many crates of chá are stacked on one of the long tables placed against a wall behind the cooks.

The Rivergrass cooks step out of the way and let the Song take over, as curious as I am. One of the local cooks points to the handled metal bowls and holds her hands out, palms up, signifying a question. The Song cook looks puzzled for a moment, then says, "Wok."

They bring in special stoves made to hold the wok, shaped like a box, with a circular opening on the top and mounted to a metal frame with sturdy legs. One of the cooks apparently asks Li for some fresh meat and vegetables. He goes in search and returns a short time later with an armful of meats, some fresh, others smoked or cured. Several of our People carry wooden boxes and canvas bags behind him. They dump the containers and Li appears to explain to the Song cooks what each local thing is. The cooks slice thin bits and taste little bites of each of the vegetables, then confer with each other.

One cook shaves several small, thin pieces of the meat, which happens to be venison, with a large rectangular knife that goes through the meat like slicing air. He gets a stove going, and I see coal is the fuel. When he is satisfied, he places the wok into the hole and waits until it starts smoking. He then pours what looks like some kind of oil into the wok and lets it heat. Finally, the meat goes in. He uses one of the special tools they brought to toss the bits of meat around. When he feels they are ready, he scoops them out of the wok and sets them on a plate.

The Song cooks gather around and wait a moment for them to be cool enough to handle. Then each takes a piece and pops it in their mouth. They chew slowly; I suppose they are releasing the flavor and analyzing it. Then they confer together. Finally, all smiles, they nod and turn to the local vegetables, tasting small thin slices of each, and they confer again. This time there's some argument, becoming heated at times, with waving arms and some shouting, all of which is great entertainment for everyone else in the lodge, especially the native cooks. Apparently they can appreciate the passion the Song bring to their art.

Finally some agreement takes place and the cooks fire up more of the stoves, and each starts preparing the ingredients. Some cooks begin to boil water. When it is rolling, with steam billowing up, they drop what looks to me like pale birds' nests into the water. A few moments later, they use another of the new tools to scoop long limp strips out, which they set aside.

The People begin whispering to each other.

"Are they worms?"

"They look like worms."

Chen hears the rumor and actually laughs. We have noticed the Song don't laugh very much, so that grabs my attention. I ask him what they are.

"*Fun*," he replies. "They are made from starchy grains that are dried and then ground very fine. One adds water, and sometimes eggs, and works them into the shape that is wanted. They are dried again into the 'nests' you saw, for storage. We have many different kinds and shapes. It can also be rolled out into sheets and cut into squares or circles, and then folded around chopped meat and vegetables, or even fruit fillings. *Báifàn* is much like a plant that grows here, which yields little starchy nodules on the roots, but *báifàn* grows like a grass and the starchy bits are seeds in tassels at the top of the plant. It is a good food: gives you energy to do things. It is the base for much Song food."

All of the work the Song apparently put into their food fascinates me. We are used to hunting for meat and gathering fruits and vegetables. Those do have to be preserved for the Fall and Winter months, but little is done to change the taste, or form, of the foods. Bannock is a versatile exception, and of course salmon can be smoked, wind dried, planked, and stewed, so these ideas aren't entirely foreign. But the Song attitude toward food is more like the efforts someone puts into learning to carve story poles and masks, or making pottery. I grasp the basic concepts easily, but the Song have gone way beyond our basic sustenance. A buzz of anticipation grows in the lodge with each new thing we see.

Meanwhile, I know the unloading continues outside, so Nosey and I drift outside again. One group of sailors is bringing wooden cages ashore, stacking them on the shaded side of the warehouse. Loud squawks and clucks from the cages gradually subside. Next they unpack rolls of wooden strips, a bit taller than a man, that are woven together with thin wire. Another batch of sailors carries painted metal posts, a bit longer than the rolls are wide.

I consult with Zizhan and he leads me, Nosey, and a group of curious others to an area inside the village, but out of the way of foot traffic. The Song have two metal tubes, apparently solid at one end, with handles on two sides. They use those to set the posts in the dirt, pounding them in. Then they unroll the wired wooden strips around the outside of the posts. Workers on the inside cut small pieces of wire and secure the fence to the posts.

They leave a man-sized gap. One man brings a frame, and they secure a piece of the fencing to it. Then they attach the gate on one side with wire, making loops, I assume, for securing the gate top and bottom on both sides, then start packing the wooden cages into the enclosure. It's a brilliant construction. All but one of the sailors exits the new pen, securing the gate behind them. The man inside starts opening the little cages. One chubby bird comes out of each, looking much like wild grouse. They don't seem inclined, or able, to fly over the top of the fence, although they do flutter their wings and squawk as they run randomly to and fro.

Excited to be out of the little boxes, I suppose. The sailor inside tosses each empty box over the fence to another man, who catches it and stacks them next to the warehouse nearby until the birds are all loose inside. The post-setting tubes, and several more rolls of wire, go into the warehouse, including the partially used roll.

Naturally, a crowd of the People has gathered to see what is going on. One of them points at the birds and asks Chen, as he is passing by, what the birds are called.

"*Ji*," is the answer. "They are a favorite food for the Song. They are easy to care for, and also give many eggs. We only kill the older females who don't lay eggs well anymore. The eggs are good fried, but they are also used in making some kinds of *fun*…or 'worms,' as you call them." He cackles. I've never heard him do that before. "The bigger ones are males. You will soon have many *ji*."

Dumbstruck, the implications overwhelm me. We will never again have to worry about bad years when the hunting or fishing is slow.

Nosey is interested, sniffing at the *ji* enclosure. His attention is noted by one of the *ji* males, who puffs up and flaps his wings at us while strutting back and forth menacingly. Nosey rises to his full height on back legs, scratching the air with his front paws as he chitters excitedly back. The *ji* cocks his head to the side, then attacks the fence with wings and claws. Nosey drops to all fours and rushes the fence, gnashing teeth bared, stopping with his nose just out of the *ji's* reach. Laughing, I give Nosey a nudge and we roam back into the lodge to share what we have learned and see what the cooks are up to now.

I assumed a canoe was immediately dispatched to Highwater at the sighting of the ships to inform them of Zahn's return, and five canoes arrive as the sun is going down. They pull up onto the shore so they don't take up any dock space. First out are Fisheagle, Hawk, and Greatheart, clearly as full of anticipation and curiosity as I am. After greetings and a quick hug for me, Hawk says, "What have you seen?"

I tell him, briefly, everything I've found out and observed, except the doorpost carving. As we reach the entrance to the lodge, I turn around to stop him.

"What do you see?"

He is pointed right at it. "Umm, the lodge. It's bigger than it was last time I was here…" He peers at the story pole. "That's us!"

I grin. "You noticed. Good for you! How do you feel about being carved into the Rivergrass lodge—at the front entrance, no less?"

His eyes are wide. "It's a great honor. I don't know why they would bother with us, but at least we are together."

Grabbing his head with both hands, I kiss him enthusiastically. "That's one reason I love you. Come on, I have lots to show you, and more new things are likely unpacked by now, since you have distracted me for some time."

He chuckles. "Show me, then!"

Fisheagle and Huckleberry, in her role as Keeper of Stories, are in the thick of the bustle inside. We enter the lodge and stop to take in the activity. Kiapelaneh sees us and starts walking our way. He stops to collect Fisheagle and Huckleberry, and then takes us out to see the *ji* enclosure. I follow along to see their reaction.

Fisheagle grasps the implications immediately. "This is food security! Some of us will still fish, but only as one part of our food supply, and that must continue because it is tradition—and the fact that we like salmon. I hope we like *ji*."

His joke receives no response from our little group, lost in our own thoughts about change.

Kiapelaneh chuckles. "That's not half of it. They bring seeds for domesticated vegetables, developed over thousands of years to their current form and flavor—don't ask me how. We will plant food gardens, like we do certain flowers now, but much larger. They will also show us how to preserve what we grow so we can store it. They do this as a matter of course. Our People will never be hungry again."

His expression turns somber. "He also brought four healers. Their medicine is as far in advance of ours as is their food. Our world changes today, my friends, or rather, it changed the day Zahn left fabrics in trade with the Haida. Their tragedy will improve the lives of all the People in this land. We will care for the Haida as soon as we can. I intend to send them regular canoes of food from what we produce."

Fisheagle concurs. "They will want for nothing so long as I remain Chief of the River People."

Greatheart clears his throat. "I must speak with these healers."

Kiapelaneh nods. "I will arrange for you to be seated next to them at the feast."

Greatheart grabs him by the arms and bows his head. He seems almost desperate to begin learning Song medicine, understandably. The small-pocks disease is weighing on many minds.

The four Song healers enter, having settled into their accommodations. A young Rivergrass woman follows closely behind them. Every once in a while she reaches out and touches one of their intensely colorful robes, and she invariably earns a mild swat from the wearer of said garment. Zahn sees the ongoing interplay, chuckles, and beckons to one of his seafarers. He whispers to him for a moment, nods toward the girl, and the man heads out the door.

A short while later, the sailor returns with a wrapped package. Zahn approaches the young woman with it. She looks up at him, her doe eyes wide as he hands her the package. She rips open the tiniest hole, collapses into a vacant chair, and stares through the small window at its contents. She abruptly snatches the package up, makes an awkward bow to Zahn, and runs out. A short time later, she reenters the main room wearing an intricately embroidered robe. Stunning by itself, it fits her perfectly, accentuating her young curves. Together, they are beauty incarnate.

Her eyes almost glow in awe of the thing and how it makes her feel. Zahn smiles happily. She approaches him, spins once, flaring the bottom of the robe, then boldly slides onto his lap. She snuggles her head on his shoulder and her ecstatic smile adds another facet to her attractiveness.

Zahn's expression cycles from pleased to uncomfortable several times, his face alternating from flushed to pale. I struggle to stifle an eruption of loud laughter as he looks to Fisheagle for guidance. The Chief shrugs, the twinkle in his eye betraying his own amusement, and he smiles reassuringly. She curls into Zahn and wraps her arms around his neck. He slides an arm gently, tentatively, around her waist to hold her securely.

Food is delivered to the chiefs' table first. The meal begins with a bowl of noodles in a hot broth, with small pieces of vegetables and meat. The dish is delivered with a flat-bottomed scoop and two wooden sticks. The scoop makes sense for the broth, but what do we do with the sticks?

I snicker when Hawk drops a bit of meat for the third time, but I can't do any better. Nosey is now under the table, having a great feast on everyone's fumbled bits.

Seeing our confusion, Chen, whose Halq̓eméylem is almost as good as Zizhan's, chuckles and stands with his bowl to demonstrate how to hold and use them. He expertly twirls up a mouthful of noodles in the bowl, pops them in his mouth, and chews happily. Still holding the sticks with thumb and two fingers, he uses the scoop for the broth.

The People struggle with the sticks. It immediately becomes clear that most of us are not going to master them in one meal. A few—notably, the weavers—start to catch on. We try to use one stick to wrap the noodles around the other one, which works but with varying levels of success. Then the cooks send out square plates of very thin slices of meat, along with shredded vegetables. They bring small cups of a thin dark sauce, rich and salty. Chen stands again and demonstrates how to pick up a slice of meat and dip it into the sauce. About half of the People use their fingers, while the rest of us struggle on with the sticks with lots of splashes and hilarity as the food falls into the sauce bowls and onto the floor.

Kiapelaneh and the People who traveled with him seem quite comfortable with the sticks. Seeing that, some of us who gave up try again. Clearly it is possible, with practice.

Chapter 64: Zahn
Evolution

It is morning, the day after making port at Rivergrass. A bit groggy after a sleepless night, a pot of chá has me functioning. I left Butterfly sleeping soundly.

I brought several farmers from the Empire and today I will join them as they evaluate this new land for food crops. Hawk, the village Chief from upriver; Li and Chen to translate and guide us; and Kiapelaneh, from the port village, are with us as well. The farmers inquire about the weather in various seasons and examine the soil very closely, even digging down to an arm's length in places.

Li guides us around the area of the village and inland. The flat land is well above the sand and flood lines. The farmers seem most pleased. Afterward we take to canoes, rowing upriver toward Highwater and land at what is left of Fishcamp. The Song farmers buzz with concern when they see the damage, but Chen explains the enemy has been defeated and is unlikely to return. Reassured, they examine the soil along the River and inland, around the fortified village of Highwater where the People have cleared the brush and trees. I am very impressed by the fortifications there, and praise Chen and Li for their design. The farmers seem much more interested in the flat ground close to the water, and the forested islands in the River itself. They taste the water and ask about flooding, which Li confirms does occur during the Spring melt, and they seem pleased with the answers. Flooding in Spring is good for some crops.

As the sun drifts toward the Sea beyond the Big Island, we return to Rivergrass and gather in the lodge. When we are all settled, with chá being delivered to the tables, Kiapelaneh speaks to everyone about the People's future.

"I have seen hillsides carved into layers of flat terraces for growing food, which would give us the ability to produce sufficient food in wide variety and quantity, not only for ourselves, but also for trade. That skill has made the Song healthier, more numerous, and wealthier as well because they have excess food to trade. This allows more free time that can be used for arts and the study of nature and the land itself, music, carving and painting, and amazing pottery, of which you have now seen a few examples. They have a system of painted symbols to represent sounds, like our picture stories but much more developed, so all the details of stories are never lost. The symbols are the same wherever you go in the Empire. Messages can be sent over long distances without losing any meaning. This is how their knowledge survives over many lifetimes, so each generation can move their people's understanding of the land and the sky forward, rather than forever repeating errors or discovering knowledge of the past. Our tradition of telling the old stories is good, but whenever an Elder dies, something may be lost.

"Imagine that we have the time and energy to pursue our passions because we will always have plenty of food and someone free to help neighbors when we need it."

Kiapelaneh shakes his head. "We are a young civilization by their standards. They are ancient, with a different land and history that has shaped them in unique ways. We heard speculation from one of their leaders that our ancestors might have come from their land, so long ago that no one remembers.

"But we also saw things that we do not want to bring home. Now, in this place, we can build the foundations of a larger society based on our values: care for each other, the land, and all of its creatures; and the special places where the spirits and our ancestors remain. We will fight to defend what we love, not to steal someone else's things. I will not criticize what others have felt they had to do. I know the People can do better, by holding our traditions sacred and caring for each other above all other motivations."

The People stand as one when he finishes speaking and roar their approval, Song voices adding to the thunder in the great lodge.

Afterword

Alliance is an important book for our time. Indigenous Peoples are finally beginning to be recognized as the original inhabitants of their various lands, and codified by the United Nations Declaration on the Rights of Indigenous Peoples. In some places their land is being returned to their care, their people entitled to all of their rights under law as First Peoples. *Alliance* explores the potential they represented in the Americas before the arrival of European conquerors, and what they might have achieved.

At the beginning of the novel, the characters and their society are portrayed as they existed at the time. I have taken the liberty of transforming the dialogue, simply for the modern reader and a larger audience. Perhaps one day, *Alliance* will be translated into Halq'eméylem or the trade tongue. Until then, English will have to do.

Along the path from villages to nation, the Alliance will confront moral and ethical choices, many of which are grappled with today in political forums. Some may startle you; others reflect issues in the news that we are still deciding.

My fervent hope for *Alliance* is that it will help an aboriginal reader imagine a different past, if only for a while. For a reader who is not indigenous, I hope it helps you to understand who these people really are and how much they lost when the Europeans arrived. Imagine what Native Peoples are capable of if old prejudices are put aside.

Apologies to the Syilx for making you the villains. Someone had to be it, and you were in the right place at the right time.

Cast of Characters

River People

Badger: warrior; Midnight's Second on the rescue mission

Boomer: hunter; Midnight's Second

Grayrabbit: refugee from the Grasslands

Clayshaper: potter; now just known as Clay

Coolwater: mother of Midnight; refugee from the Grasslands

Copperflower: friend of Seabird

Coyote: hunter

Fisheagle: Chief of the River People

Freebird: Hawk's sister

Greatheart: healer

Hawk: hunter; Chief of Highwater

Huckleberry: Keeper of Stories

Kestrel: warrior

Longarm: Watch Commander

Lynx: warrior

Maskmaker: carver

Midnight: refugee of the Grasslands; daughter of Coolwater; Warleader

Nighthawk: hunter

Nosey: a raccoon; companion of Midnight

Sage: friend of Seabird

Screech-Owl: warrior

Seabird: hunter; Hawk's Second

Sharpstick: Boomer's father

Smallwave: Hawk's mother

Sparrow: Grassland hunter; now a slave

Sundog: hunter

Sunshine: coppersmith

Weaver: from Clearwater Village

Windflower: Midnight's sister; refugee from the Grasslands

Woodfern: friend of Seabird; apprentice Keeper of Stories

Woodshaper: a carver; Midnight's father; refugee from the Grasslands

Rivergrass People

Kiapelaneh: Rivergrass Chief

Grasslands People

Fishhawk: hunter

Hardspear: Shaman's new Chief

Shaman: murderer of the Grassland Chief

Willowspear: hunter

Haida

Ts'aak: Trader; Chief of the Haida

The Song

Chen: Song advisor to Rivergrass

Dù: Song advisor to the Haida; later, his name changes to Darkwater

Li: Song advisor to Rivergrass

Wei: Song advisor to River People

Zahn: Captain of a Song trade ship

Zizhan: Song advisor to River People

Made in the USA
Monee, IL
06 February 2021